PRAISE FOR THE DRAMA HIGH SERIES

"You'll definitely feel for Jayd Jackson, the bold sixteen-year-old Compton, California, junior at the center of keep-it-real Drama High stories."
—*Essence* magazine on *Drama High: Jayd's Legacy*

"Compton native and Drama High author L. Divine writes a fascinating story capturing the voice of young black America."
—*The Cincinnati Herald* on the Drama High series

"Filled with all the elements that make for a good book—young love, non-stop drama and a taste of the supernatural, it is sure to please."
—THE RAWSISTAZ Reviewers on *Drama High: The Fight*

"If you grew up on a steady diet of saccharine-*Sweet Valley* novels and think there aren't enough books specifically for African American teens, you're in luck."
—*Prince George's Sentinel* on *Drama High: The Fight*

"Through a healthy mix of book smarts, life experiences, and down-to-earth flavor, L. Divine has crafted a well-nuanced coming-of-age tale for African-American youth."
—*The Atlanta Voice* on *Drama High: The Fight*

"*Drama High* has it all . . . fun, fast, addictive."
—Cara Lockwood, bestselling author of *Moby Clique*

Also by L. Divine

THE FIGHT

SECOND CHANCE

JAYD'S LEGACY

FRENEMIES

LADY J

COURTIN' JAYD

Published by Kensington Publishing Corporation

Drama High, Vol. 7
HUSTLIN'

L. Divine

KENSINGTON PUBLISHING CORP.
www.kensingtonbooks.com

To Assata and Ajani: your very existence makes my hustle tight. To Karen, Lesleigh, Darla, Veleece, Selena, Adeola, and everyone else on the front lines at Dafina/Kensington: thank you all for hustling hard on Drama High's behalf. To Brendan and his team at Objective Entertainment: thank you for hustling hard on my behalf. To my parents and godparents: thank you for your faith, love, and dedication always. To all of the hard working, single parents out there: keep on keeping on, and remember our blessings come from our children. And finally, to everyone who's working consistently to make it to the next level no matter where they're at in life: keep hustling and always have faith in your flow~

THE CREW

Jayd

A sassy sixteen-year-old from Compton, California, who comes from a long line of Louisiana conjure women. She is the only one in her lineage born with brown eyes and a caul. Her grandmother appropriately named her "Jayd," which is also the name her grandmother took on in her days as a voodoo queen in New Orleans. She lives with her grandparents, four uncles, and her cousin Jay. Jayd is in all AP classes and visits her mother on the weekend. She has a tense relationship with her father, whom she sees occasionally, and has never-ending drama in her life, whether at school or home.

Mama/Lynn Mae

When Jayd gets in over her head, her grandmother, Mama, is always there to help her. A full-time conjure woman with magical green eyes and a long list of both clients and haters, Mama also serves as Jayd's teacher, confidante, and protector.

Mom/Lynn Marie

At thirty-something years old, Lynn Marie would never be mistaken for a mother of a teenager. But Jayd's mom is definitely all that and with her green eyes, she keeps the men guessing. Able to talk to Jayd telepathically, Lynn Marie is always there when Jayd needs her.

Esmeralda

Mama's nemesis and Jayd's nightmare, this next-door neighbor is anything but friendly. She relocated to Compton from Louisiana around the same time Mama did and has been a thorn in Mama's side ever since. She continuously causes trouble for Mama and Jayd, interfering with Jayd's school life through Misty, Mrs. Bennett, and Jeremy's mom. Esmeralda's cold blue eyes have powers of their own, although not nearly as powerful as Mama's.

Rah

Rah is Jayd's first love from junior high school who has come back into her life when a mutual friend, Nigel, transfers from Rah's high school (Westingle) to South Bay. He knows everything about her and is her spiritual confidant. Rah lives in Los Angeles but grew up with his grandparents in Compton like Jayd. He loves Jayd fiercely but has a girlfriend who refuses to go away (Trish) and a baby-mama (Sandy). Rah is a hustler by necessity and a music producer by talent. He takes care of his younger brother Kamal and holds the house down while his dad is locked up and his mother strips at a local club.

Misty

The word "frenemies" was coined for this former best friend of Jayd's. Misty has made it her mission to sabotage Jayd any way she can. Living around the corner from Jayd, she has the unique advantage of being an original hater from the neighborhood and at school.

KJ

He's the most popular basketball player on campus, Jayd's ex-boyfriend, and Misty's current boyfriend. Ever since he and Jayd broke up, he's made it his personal mission to persecute her.

Nellie

One of Jayd's best friends, Nellie is the prissy princess of the crew. She is also dating Chance, even though it's Nigel she's really feeling. Nellie made history at South Bay by becoming the first Black Homecoming princess and has let the crown go to her head.

Mickey

The gangster girl of Jayd's small crew. She and Nellie are best friends but often at odds with each other, mostly because Nellie secretly wishes she could be more like Mickey. A true hood girl, she loves being from Compton and her man with no name is a true gangster.

Jeremy

A first for Jayd, Jeremy is her white ex-boyfriend who also happens to be the most popular cat at South Bay. Rich, tall and extremely handsome, Jeremy's witty personality and good conversation keep Jayd on her toes and give Rah a run for his money—literally.

Mickey's Man

Never using his name, Mickey's original boyfriend is a trouble-maker and always hot on Mickey's trail. Always in and out of jail, Mickey's man is notorious in her hood for being a cold-hearted gangster, and loves to be in control. He also has a thing for Jayd but Jayd can't stand to be anywhere near him.

Nigel

The new quarterback on the block, Nigel is a friend of Jayd's from junior high and also Rah's best friend, making Jayd's world even smaller at South Bay High. Nigel is the star foot-ball player and dumped his ex-girlfriend at Westingle (Tasha) to be with his new baby-mama to be, Mickey. Jayd is caught up in the mix as both of their friends, but her loyalty lies with Nigel because she's known him longer and he's always had her back.

Chance

The rich white hip-hop kid of the crew, Chance is Jayd's drama homie and Nellie's boyfriend, if you let him tell it. He used to have a crush on Jayd and now has turned his attention to Nellie.

Bryan

The youngest of Mama's children and Jayd's favorite uncle, Bryan is a dj by night and works at the local grocery store during the day. He's also an acquaintance of both Rah and KJ from playing ball around the hood. Bryan often gives Jayd helpful advice about her problems with boys and hating girls alike. Out of all of Jayd's uncles, Bryan gives her grandparents the least amount of trouble.

Jay

Jay is more like an older brother to Jayd than her cousin. Like Jayd, he lives with Mama but his mother (Mama's youngest daughter) left him when he was a baby and never returned. He doesn't know his father and attends Compton High. He and Jayd often cook together and help Mama around the house.

Prologue

After playing ball all day I'd think Rah would be exhausted, but he's actually hyped from beating KJ and his boys in overtime. I enjoyed watching my boys stomp KJ's ego. If I'm not mistaken, I think I saw KJ shed a tear he was so pissed. I can't wait to see the look on his face at school tomorrow because me and my girls are letting everyone know KJ got his assed whipped, even if it was off campus. I know KJ thinks I had something to do with him losing and for once, he's right. But if Misty still thinks it's my fault she and KJ have the clap she's crazier than I ever gave her credit for.

I'm exhausted if for no other reason than because I had to deal with two crazy broads who are after Rah and Misty's hating ass all weekend long. Even if Rah's not my man anymore, I still have to fight with two of his ex-girlfriends over him. And thanks to Misty being my former best friend, everyone knows more about my business than they should. It's one thing to have my school enemies at school and my home enemies at home, but when they come together the outcome can only be negative for me. I'm going to need to give myself a cleansing after the long weekend we just had. My drama repellant also needs some tinkering and I hope my grandmother's up for the task. I can handle Rah's current leach,

Trish—his latest ex who just won't go away—and Misty always. But his baby-mama, Sandy, being up in the picture is more than I can bear alone.

Sandy remembers a little about how my grandmother and I get down, but she and I weren't friends long enough to get too close, unlike Misty and I. I befriended Sandy on her first day at my old school, Family Christian. Even though she's a year ahead of Rah and me in school, and two years ahead of us in age, she jumped Rah the first chance she got and made me her enemy soon after. I didn't know as much about my gifts then as I do now, and I'll be damned if Sandy's going to wreak havoc in my life again like she did two years ago.

This has been the longest ten minutes of my life and there's so much traffic on Crenshaw from the Sunday night cruising that we're stuck with each other for longer than usual. Rah and I haven't spoken a word since he told me about his plan to sue Sandy for sole custody of their little girl because I don't know what else to say. What he doesn't know is that I had a dream about Sandy leaving two years ago, but I never told him or Mama about it because, honestly, I didn't want her to stay.

On one hand, I'm glad Rah's ready to take full responsibility for his daughter. Sandy did keep her away from him for almost two years without so much as a phone call and she's not the most stable person in the world. But Rah has enough on his plate as it is. He's only a junior and he already takes care of his little brother and holds down the household while his mom strips all day and night. Raising a toddler will be more than he can handle and I'm afraid of him doing whatever he deems necessary to hold it down, including more shit that could land his ass in lockdown with his father.

"What are you over there thinking about?" Rah asks, turning down the smooth oldies he's playing on his car stereo.

Before I can answer him, Rah's phone vibrates again and this time he answers. He better not be talking to either one of his broads in front of me right now because I'm not in a very friendly mood. Rah's really got me worried about his next move and he seems too in control of everything, especially when it comes to Sandy and his baby girl.

"Who's that?" I ask softly, not wanting to be too rude but letting him know I won't be ignored. Rah looks at me out of the corner of his eye and then back at the bumper-to-bumper traffic facing us. We haven't moved more than three feet in the last five minutes and it doesn't look like it's going to get any better anytime soon. Whoever's on the phone is making him smile, so I know it can't be one of his other girls.

"Yeah, Nigel, we're right around the corner from your spot, man. We'll be there in five minutes." Rah hangs up his cell and throws it on my lap before giving me a sarcastic grin. "Here. Now you can monitor all of my calls." He smiles at me and puts his blinker on, ready to cross traffic. But because he's not in a classic pimped-out ride, no one takes him seriously.

"Very funny," I say, tossing the phone into his lap. I'm glad he's got jokes because I need a good laugh right about now. Rah and I have been way too serious lately. I'm glad I have him to talk to about both the good and bad in our lives, but what happened to my cool kicking-it companion? Good kissing messes everything up. I should have learned that lesson by now.

"Is it cool if we roll by Nigel's spot? They're having a little session to continue the celebration." After we left Pann's stuffed like a holiday turkey, we went back to my mom's and grabbed my stuff so I could get back to Compton earlier than usual. My mom hasn't made it back from Lake Tahoe yet and I still have much work to do. But kicking it with my friends is always a priority, even if my girls still aren't currently speaking to each other. Maybe a session is just what we need to chill us all out.

"You know I've got to get back to Mama's soon," I say, looking at the clock on the dashboard. It's always nice spending the weekends with my mom, but it's back to reality during the week. Maybe one day my mom will be able to handle having me full-time, but I've already asked her several times and the answer's always no. "It's already after five." I usually get home around seven on Sundays and I don't want to give Mama any reason to be irritated with me. If I come home smelling like weed she'll grill me like I was the one smoking, even though she knows me better than that.

"Yeah, I know, girl. And I still have to pick up Kamal from my grandmother's house, so we'll just kick it for a minute, cool?"

I nod my head in agreement as he turns down Slauson Avenue heading toward Nigel's pad. I can't help but wonder how my girls are getting along and whether or not Nellie's in a forgiving mood. She and Mickey ignored each other during the game and at lunch, but at least Nellie kept her mouth shut about Mickey's baby-daddy decision. I hope it stays that way until things cool down a bit because I'd hate to see what would happen if Nellie wanted to give Mickey a taste of her own bitchy medicine. That's a gift no one should have to accept.

~ 1 ~
Misgiving

"Can't you tell the way they have to mention/
How they helped you out, you're such a hopeless victim."

—LAURYN HILL

When we get to Nigel's house I can see Chance's Nova and Nigel's Impala in the driveway. As nice as their classic cars are they should've been the ones cruising down Crenshaw this evening. I guess Nigel's parents are out for the night, leaving us to chill alone in his beautiful home. Nigel lives in a huge old house in Lafayette Square that his parents recently had renovated when they relocated from Compton two years ago. His older sister is away at Spelman, so it's just him and his parents and they give Nigel all of the freedom he could ever ask for.

When we walk into the foyer the bright chandelier hanging from the ceiling sparkles, sending rainbow rays from the setting sun across the white walls. We step down the few steps and into the main room, which serves as both a living room and entertainment area with a minibar in the back corner.

"Come on in and make yourselves at home. We're up in my room," Nigel says, closing the door behind us as I follow Rah up the stairs. The houses on this side of Los Angeles have been here forever, and the white folks are moving back in and attempting to buy them up, even if they are only a stone's throw away from the hood. Daddy calls it gentrification. I call it hood jacking. They're moving back to Compton, too. But it's going to take a lot longer for them to take our streets back over, unlike here in the big city.

"Where are the folks?" Rah asks as Nigel swoops past us to open his bedroom door, letting us into his private fortress away from the rest of the house. From the looks of it, the other three rooms on this floor are still in the process of being remodeled. When we walk into his room the pungent aroma of incense mixed with tobacco and other smoke hits me. Damn, now the shit's going to be all in my hair. I may have to sport it wet all week if the smell's too much for me.

"Oh, they had some sort of fundraiser at the community center off Vernon and Manchester. You know my dad can't resist getting a pat on the back for writing a check even if he wouldn't normally be caught dead on that side of the hood." Nigel's dad used to play professional basketball, but retired early after a knee injury. Now his dad is a top executive at a sports gear company and his mom's a not-so-happy house-wife.

"What's up, y'all," I say through the cloud of smoke in the large room.

Nigel's room is off the chain. Even Jeremy would be envi-ous of his sports-themed room that is at least the size of the living room downstairs. There is an aquarium like the one at Rah's house, a king-sized bed in the center of the room, and two futons on opposite walls, which are now occupied by Nellie and Chance on one and Nigel and Mickey spread out across the other. Rah and I take a seat at the card table oppo-site the entertainment center, ready for a quick chill.

"That was a good game, man. Thanks for letting my boy play," Chance says in between puffs. "What's up with you, Jayd?"

If I didn't know better I'd say that Nellie has been smok-ing, too, but I'm sure it's just a contact high.

"Nothing much. Just ready to get back on my grind." I can

only relax so much when I know I have mad work waiting on me at home. This is why I must get my own ride, and soon. I hate being at the mercy of other folks, even when we are chilling. When I'm ready to roll I don't want to have to ask anyone. And, by the looks of it, we may be here for a minute longer than I want to be.

"How's your leg?" I ask Chance as he passes the blunt to Nigel.

"It's cool. Just a little sore."

Rah's looking down at his vibrating phone. The way his jawbone just tightened up I'd say it was probably Sandy. As long as he doesn't answer in front of me we're good.

"You should've seen Nellie's prissy ass trying to get away from the gunshots without messing up her hair. It was hilarious," Mickey says, making us all laugh. But Nellie doesn't find it amusing at all.

"At least I take my health and well-being seriously, unlike you, mommy-to-be."

There was more venom in that comment than in a poisonous snakebite. The two of them have been hating on each other more and more lately and I'm sick of it. I wish Mickey would just come clean so we can move on from being full-time secret keepers and back to best friends chilling.

"Taking care of myself means getting out of dangerous situations I may find myself in," Mickey says, adjusting herself on Nigel's lap. "It's called street smarts, baby girl. And no, there's no book you can run and buy to teach them to you. You've got to live it to be it."

Nellie looks like she's about to burst with anger. It's been an extra long day and I can't deal with another fight.

"Okay ladies, that's enough," Chance says, feeling my pain. "Where's the blunt? Let's get this vibe mellowed out." Chance looks at Nellie, ready to laugh at her until he realizes she's not joking.

"Y'all shouldn't smoke around Mickey. She's expecting," Nellie says.

I knew Nellie would be Mickey's nightmare of an auntie and from the look on Mickey's face, she's had about all she can take from our girl for one day.

"Nellie, sit down and shut up," Mickey says, taking the blunt from Nigel and licking it, just to irritate Nellie even more. "Every pregnant chick I know is around weed twenty-four seven and their babies come out just fine."

"Are you going to let her do that? She's carrying your baby!" Nellie screams at Nigel, who's way too high to take her tantrum seriously.

But Mickey's completely sober, and now she's also completely pissed off. "Mind your business, Nellie."

"It is my business, Mickey."

I feel like a kitten watching a tennis match. I look from Mickey to Nellie and back again, knowing they want to rip into each other right now.

Before I can stop her, Nellie lets the cat out of the bag. "Mickey's not sure who the baby-daddy is and chose you, Nigel, because you're going to be ballin' one day."

So much for Nellie holding her tongue and allowing us a chill ending to our victorious weekend.

"One day? Baby, if you haven't noticed, I'm ballin' now," Nigel says, pretending to shoot another basket.

Rah looks at me as if to say *it's time to roll,* and I couldn't agree with him more. We've both had enough drama for one day.

"Did you hear what I just said?" Nellie shouts, stepping up to Nigel as Mickey steps up to her. "You may not be the father of Mickey's baby." As the words sink in, Mickey looks from Nigel to Nellie waiting for the next move. Chance, Rah and I wait in silence.

"What happens between me and Mickey is between me

and Mickey." Nigel looks down at his girl, who looks victoriously at our girl. Nellie looks around the room and feels humiliated. I told her this would happen. She runs outside fuming and Chance is right behind her.

"Man, I've got to pick up my brother. I'll holler at you later," Rah says. "Jayd, you ready?"

Man, am I glad that's over for now. "Yeah. See y'all at school tomorrow."

As we walk out of the garage I look in the driveway to see Nellie and Chance talking in his car. Knowing my girls, there's going to be some drama to follow in the morning. I know Nellie thinks she was trying to help, but that's the problem with giving people things they don't want: they have the right to throw them back in your face no matter if they needed it or not.

"How was your weekend, baby?" Mama asks, rolling over in her bed and sitting up under her blankets. The floor heater in the hallway has to heat up the entire house and Mama likes to keep the door closed, which makes it pretty chilly in here at night. We used to sleep with a portable heater on the floor in between our matching beds, but Mama had a dream about it catching her bed on fire and got rid of that and her electric blanket just to be on the safe side.

"It was okay. How was yours?" I ask, plopping down on my made bed and placing my backpack, purse and weekend bag down beside me. It'll be so nice to have my own room one day. But I must admit, I'm happy to be home. My mom's couch gets a little uncomfortable after a couple of nights and with the long weekend we just had, my back is screaming for my tiny bed.

"You know, Jayd, I just finished working at that shelter all week like I do every year, on what I refer to as the misgiving holiday, and they already asked me back for Christmas. And not only do they want me back to help serve, they also want me to donate one hundred of my prosperity gris-gris. Now mind you, I just donated twenty-five of them to several of the guests, including Pam, who should be dropping by tomorrow afternoon if she remembers," Mama says, referring to the neighborhood crackhead she feeds on a regular basis.

"Wow, one hundred," I say. I've only made a few of the infamous charm bags myself and one can take me all night. I can't imagine making as many as Mama does on a regular basis. "Are you going to make them?" I ask as I unpack the items in my weekend bag and spread them across my bed, organizing it all into tiny piles. There's a pile for my toiletries, dirty clothes and clean clothes.

"Hell no, I'm not going to make them," Mama replies, looking at me and my stuff over her glasses as she eyes my inventory. I know Mama goes through my things when I'm not at home. I can tell by the way everything's so neatly folded when I return and I've never cared that much about avoiding creases. That's why I keep all of the important stuff—like letters from Mickey and Nellie—in my locker at school.

"I don't see why you even go to the shelter in the first place. Don't you get tired of helping people for free?"

Mama looks at me like I'm someone else's child, not the granddaughter she practically raised from birth. "Never, Jayd, never. What I do get tired of is being taken for granted by those I do choose to help. I can see why Netta sticks to doing hair. Being a full-time priestess is no joke," she says, taking a small, open container off of the nightstand and rubbing her special menthol and eucalyptus shea butter ointment on her hands.

"Yeah, but there has to be a better way to help folks than getting run down while you do."

"I feel you, girl, and trust me. There are those days when I want to throw this book at some of my clients, literally."

Mama points at the large spirit book. If she hit someone with that it would knock them out instantly. "But that's why we are here, Jayd, especially those of us who can help. It's when we give to people who don't appreciate our efforts or when we give for the wrong reasons that we get in trouble."

"I hear you loud and clear," I say as I reflect on Nellie's unsolicited news this afternoon. I begin to take out my homework that didn't get finished over the holiday weekend. "I hate when they make us do assignments on Thanksgiving. What is there really to be thankful about when discussing the actual holiday?"

Why did I say that out loud? Now Mama's really going to go off.

"That's why I call Thanksgiving the misgiving holiday. Only in this country can you have a national holiday that's supposed to be about joy and being thankful for what you've got, based on the massacre of the natives who were here before the Europeans arrived. As long as Queen Califia was here before Cortez and his men showed up, they never had to break bread with people they didn't want to."

Mama can't stand any of the commercialized holidays, except for Christmas—which she's changed into her own holiday, much to the disapproval of my grandfather. But Daddy knows better than to mess with Mama, especially when it comes to her spirit work.

"I feel you, Mama. People make too big a deal about the holidays anyway. I like the way we celebrate Eshu on Christmas Eve and our ancestors on Christmas Day." Truth be told, it's feels no different, especially since the entire family gathers on Christmas Eve like we always have. The only difference is that being that he's a full-time pastor, Daddy says his prayers and Mama says hers.

"I hope you understand why studying about your ancestors is so important, Jayd. We give because it's a large part of who we are, never because we expect something in return. Be just as leery of people who give because they want to be thanked for it as you are of people who want more of what you give without giving anything in return. Either attitude is the opposite of good character and that shit doesn't fly in my book. Your ancestors can testify to that mistake."

Yes they can, all of them.

"Speaking of ancestors, I'm doing my report in government class on Queen Califia."

Mama looks at me with that coy smile of hers I only get when she's extremely pleased with my growing crown. "I'm proud of you, girl. I know that wasn't an easy topic to choose at your school." Mama reaches over to grab the spirit book from the shrine. She must've been using it tonight because it's usually in the spirit room out back or in the kitchen. "Did you get all of the information out of here you need to get started?" Mama thumbs through the aged pages of the over-sized book. Every family should have one of these to keep up with their lineage.

"Yes, I did. And I also have a teacher at school who may be able to help."

She stops browsing and looks me dead in the eye. Her green eyes shimmer as she probes my sight, trying to see what I see. I know she can if she really wants to, but I'd prefer she ask instead. "A teacher at South Bay High that knows about the Black Queen of California and our Golden State's namesake. Really?" Mama sounds more interested than I expected. It's not like Califia's that big of a secret. And besides, I think the story of her and her people may be one of the original misgiving tales to tell.

"Yeah, Mr. Adewale. He's the latest addition to the faculty roster and he's not bad on the eyes either," I say, folding my clean clothes, ready to take them into to Daddy's room to store in the closet. I can wash the dirty ones while I'm in the spiritroom working on my homework. I'd better get to work now if want to be in bed by a decent hour. It's going to be hard waking up at five-thirty in the morning after not having to for several days.

"Mr. Adewale," Mama says as the name rolls off her tongue like syrup. It's almost as if she's recalling something, but I can't tell what. My skills aren't nearly as tight as Mama's. "Uh huh. Don't you think you have enough boy trouble as it is?" she asks, again reading my mind. But as strong as my vibe is, I think anyone can tell I'm feeling Mr. A. "Speaking of which, how is Rah? Did you have a good time with him on Thanksgiving?"

"Well, I actually spent the day with Nellie, Chance, and Jeremy," I say, leaving out the part about us having dinner at Pann's on Thanksgiving. Details aren't that important, especially not the ones that are going to get me yelled at.

"Where was Rah?"

I return Mama's stare from across the small room and take a deep breath. I don't feel like getting into our long weekend filled with baby-mama drama and hating girlfriends. But I can't lie to Mama about it all if I want to get to work anytime soon.

"He was visiting his daughter."

Mama's curious look quickly morphs into a concerned frown as she remembers the pain I went through with Rah and Sandy. More importantly, she remembers the prayers we did for Rah to get his daughter back. Sandy ran off with their baby when she was only a few weeks old and hasn't looked back since.

"How is the baby? She must be almost two by now, right?" I know Mama wants to go off, but she spares my feelings and doesn't grill me any further about Rah and I do appreciate it.

"She's fine, I guess."

From my response, Mama can tell I haven't seen his

daughter, and rolls her eyes. I know there's still a lot of mess and unfinished business between Rah and me regarding his baby girl, and I intend to get on it as soon as I can. I've got to tighten my hustle if I'm going to make it through Mickey's pregnancy and through this battle between Rah and Sandy over their daughter. I also want to give myself the best Kwanza gift of all: a car. And it's all going to take some serious hustling on my part.

~ 2 ~

The Art of Hustling

"Some of them want to use you/
Some of them want to get used by you."

—EURYTHMICS

It never ceases to amaze me how quickly one holiday runs into the other. Mama says there was a time when Halloween was Halloween and Christmas was Christmas. Now Santa hats are put out with the pumpkins, and it throws me off every year. Speaking of throwing, Misty heads my way with the rest of her sometimey crew right beside her. KJ and her are back on point, I see, and Shae and Tony look as high as ever. The first bell hasn't even rung yet and these fools already need to escape.

"Hey, Jayd," KJ says, chewing on a toothpick, with one arm around Misty and the other one holding his backpack. They all turn the corner, heading toward the main office a few steps in front of me.

I'm surprised KJ has the nerve to speak to me after his humiliating loss this weekend and his punk-ass attitude afterwards. Talk about a sore loser.

"I told you not to talk to her. And don't look directly into her eyes, either," Misty says, repeating something that sounds more like my neighbor Esmeralda than herself.

Oh, this should be an interesting day. Just when I thought my walk up the main path to the front of South Bay High couldn't get any more difficult, Reid and Laura walk outside of the front doors, stapling the Fall Festival fliers to the front bulletin board. I stop and see my name next to Reid's name in the lead roles. I still can't believe I'm playing opposite him as Lady Macbeth. That's some serious irony for my ass.

"There's my old lady now," Reid jokes as KJ and followers walk past them into the main office with me not far behind.

"You wish," I say, passing him and his actual girlfriend as I head into the main office with the rest of the crowd.

Christmas decorations are being spun up above our heads giving the place a very festive vibe. The six-foot Christmas tree is standing in the corner by the principal's office. The athletes and cheerleaders will have the pleasure of decorating that gaudy thing while ASB gets to do everything else. By the end of the week the entire campus will look like Santa's village, minus the snow.

"Oh Jayd, please. The only reason they gave you the part was to avoid hearing your racist bull," Laura says, spewing more toxins with every word.

This chick is more serious about this part than I am. Ain't nothing worse than a hating white girl.

"Damn, Laura. Are you afraid of losing your man to Jayd or something?" Chance asks, entering the hall to have my back. Jeremy, Matt and Seth are also approaching the main office through the main hall entrance. I wish he wouldn't have said that. Laura's already on fire and I don't need anyone adding gasoline to the mix.

"As if," Laura says, flipping her long brown hair over her left shoulder. She wouldn't be bad looking if her attitude wasn't so funky. "Reid has good taste, and eyes for me only."

Now even Laura can't be that stupid. I wouldn't trust any dude to have eyes for me only. If a fool tells me that, I know he's trying to get his game on and I'm not buying it. KJ used to say that shit to me—and the rest of his broads—all of the time. He's probably feeding that bull to Misty as we speak, and even Misty can't be deluded enough to fall for that line.

"Well then, stop hating on her for getting the part. Suck it up, Laura. Jayd's an actress and you're just a fake." Chance puts his arm around my shoulders and smiles at a steaming Reid. If Chance could sock Reid in his jaw without suffering any repercussions, I'm sure he would. I'd even be tempted to get a punch in myself if the circumstances were right.

"What business is it of yours, Chance? I thought you were dating the other one," Reid says as Jeremy, Matt, and Seth join us. Only my girls and Nigel are missing from the scene. Tony and Shae are watching from the background, as usual, while Misty and KJ stand front and center, much more obvious about their eavesdropping.

"The other one what?" Jeremy asks. He doesn't need a reason to argue with Reid. The ongoing feud between their families is enough ammunition to last him a lifetime. I still can't believe they hate each other because their older brothers used to date the same girl, but it's as real as the beef between Mama and our neighbor Esmeralda and can be just as dangerous when provoked.

"The other friend," Reid says, chickening out of completing his racist statement, but we all know what he meant.

"Yeah right, Reid. If anyone's crying some racist crap it's the two of you," Chance says, releasing his hold on me as Nellie and Mickey both approach the tense meeting from opposite directions. I wonder how Nellie got to school this morning, because I know she didn't ask Mickey for a ride.

Jeremy turns around and looks in the same direction as Chance and I. He looks back at the two of us and smiles, like he senses something's going on between us. I know Jeremy knows better than that. I'll have to ask him what that's all about during third period. But right now we have to get out of here and get to first period before we're all tardy.

"Whatever, Slim Shady. We know where your loyalties lie," Laura says to Chance. Seeing Mickey approach, the self-proclaimed new queen bee of the rich-bitch crew decides to tone down her attitude and head for the ASB room. I would go over there myself to holla at Ms. Toni before the day begins, but I'll wait until the coast is clear of her nosy students.

"What did you just call me?" Chance says, ready to step up to Laura like she's a dude: some girls bring that out in a dude. I live in a house full of men, so I know when to shut up, as my mom would say. It's not that I'm afraid of a dude because I'm not. But sometimes enough is enough, and Laura just ran out with Chance.

"You heard me. You haven't been white since junior high," she says, making Reid and KJ both laugh. They all went to school together. I'm sure it's true but damn, she didn't have to go there with him in front of a crowd like that.

I can't let my boy catch the heat I'm supposed to be taking. I'd better put a stop to this before things get out of hand.

"This is between you and me, Laura. But as usual, you'd rather take cheap shots at my friends than fight your own battle," I say, redirecting her attention back to me. The bell rings above our heads as the rest of the folks in the crowded hall pick up the pace. Like them, I'm ready to get on with this day as well. And the sooner I can shut Laura up, the better.

"You're right Jayd. This is between you and me. Remember that when this comes back to bite you in your fat ass." Laura walks through the double doors Reid's holding open for her.

Who's she calling fat?

"I like your ass," Jeremy says, making everyone still present laugh at Laura's semi-dramatic exit.

I still can't help but feel something more is up with Laura. That last look she gave me sent chills down my spine and that's highly unusual. I wonder what she's got up her sleeve this time, and who's helping her deal her wicked hand?

"That skinny bitch deserves a slap in the face. Y'all should write that into the script," Mickey says to Matt and Seth, who both look as if they're still waking up. Jeremy's entire crew usually surfs in the morning, followed by a smoke-out session before coming to school. Living five minutes away from campus must be nice in more ways than one.

"Yeah, I'd come see that play," Nellie says, leading the way into the buzzing hall. She's still pissed at Mickey for lying to Nigel and getting away with it. But after Laura and Tania treated her like a maidservant during Homecoming, she can't stand the broad either. I don't know how she puts up with having to work side-by-side with Laura and Reid for ASB projects. Their stuck-up attitudes can be highly contagious. I'm just glad they haven't gotten to Nellie.

"You're still coming to opening night to support your folks though, right?" Chance says, causing Nellie to raise her eyebrows and Jeremy's cheeks to flush.

What the hell's up with these two and their unfounded jealousy? Even if Chance and I had crushes on each other last year, we're just friends now. Don't they know I have enough boy drama to deal with as it is?

"I don't know," Nellie says, twirling her freshly-pressed hair around her index finger before letting the loose curls fall over her shoulder. I would love to get my hands on her head full of hair. A head cleansing would do her tight ass some good. "There are only a few shopping days left until Christmas and I have a lot on my to-do list to check off still."

Chance looks hurt that Nellie would even entertain not coming to his opening night, and they're supposed to be dating. Even if I think he should say something to Nellie, I doubt he rocks the boat, especially as hard as he fought to get a ride in it.

"Well, we'll be there. Ain't that right, baby," Nigel says, tightly holding a glowing Mickey around her expanding waist.

I don't know if she's trying to hide her pregnancy from the rest of the school, but she won't be able to for much longer. Her Baby Phat jeans are popping at the seams already and I don't think Kimora makes maternity clothes. I wonder what Mickey will be sporting for the next seven months?

"It depends. Will there be food?" Mickey asks while chewing on a Red Vine.

Nellie looks at our girl in total disgust. Mickey and her cravings. I hope her baby is as big as she's going to be now that she's eating for two all day long.

"It's a play, not a movie," Seth says, crossing his lanky arms across his chest and rolling his eyes behind his Versace shades. He gets pissed when people don't take his theater seriously. Matt is more nonchalant about it, but the two of them take care of the sets, so they are more particular about what goes on inside the drama studio than any of the other students in the drama class or club.

"But people have been known to sneak in food, and there will be refreshments for sale during the intermission." Matt looks bored by the conversation and starts to lead the way into the main hall where our lockers are.

I feel for the freshmen and sophomore students having their lockers outside, especially when it rains. I'm glad to be a junior, even though we're only going into the third month of school, and the year has already been filled with drama.

"Bet. We'll hit up the liquor store before we roll through, but we'll be there for sure," Mickey says, allowing Nigel to wrap her up tightly in his arms and walk her toward her locker.

Nellie, obviously annoyed by their affectionate behavior, walks off to her locker, which is only three doors down from Mickey's, leaving Chance to run after her, as usual.

I can't understand why Chance allows Nellie to use him like she does. I guess having some attention from Nellie is better than receiving none at all. And I know Nellie hates on Mickey for her magnificent pimping, but Nellie ain't too far behind in her game. The major difference between my girls is that Nellie's jealousy is going to get the best of her if she's not careful.

"I'll catch up with y'all later," Chance says, leaving me and Jeremy alone.

Damn, this is more than a bit uncomfortable, especially after our kiss on Sunday. Sensing my uneasiness, Jeremy breaks the ice. I didn't get a chance to call him back yesterday, but I am wearing the puka-shell necklace under my pink hoodie, as well as my gold bangle he gave me a while back. I know he can feel me feeling him.

"So what's up with you? I looked for you at the bus stop, but I guess I was too slow this morning, huh?"

Jeremy's smile warms me up, even if I do still need to purchase a proper winter coat. I do this every year, hoping the cold won't come, but that never seems to work, and in the meantime I'm left with frostbite. I play with the puka shells around my neck, unsure of what to say next. I purposely took the long way around campus this morning to avoid running into Jeremy. His kiss has caused enough questions in my head. I don't need more interaction with him to further cloud my view.

"Nothing much. Just recouping from the long weekend. And you?"

I watch the other students walking by and some of them are looking at us and talking among themselves. I guess Jeremy and I will always be a hot topic to outsiders. I wonder if the same people that bet on us breaking up also placed bets on us getting back together?

"Oh, I just slept away the rest of the night, hoping my phone would ring." He closes my locker door and takes my books for me as he shoots me a devious smile. He continues to walk me to the end of the hall before passing my books back to me and looking me in the eyes. "I'm not going anywhere, Jayd. Just know that," he says, bending down to give me a kiss on the cheek before walking off toward his first period, as the rest of the students in the crowded hall buzz around us. I wish I could honestly say the same thing.

"I know," I say softly, while holding my pecked cheek and exiting the main hall out of the main entrance leading outside.

I love how most of our classrooms are located in the various corridors outside of the main building, except when it rains.

The first bell has already rung and neither of us wants to be late. I wish I had more time to kick it at lunch or break this week, but I have to work on my English portfolio before our AP meetings this week, and I still have to finish my government paper on Queen Califia, not to mention the mandatory drama rehearsal. I guess I won't be enjoying any free time this week if I want to stay on my A game.

It's a clear, crisp morning and everyone's dressed for the cold in his or her own way. Some of these beach folks are even wearing shorts and skirts. I know they have to be cold because I'm feeling the chill for them. The view of the ocean is unobstructed, tempting even me to go to the beach this morning. If only life was that simple.

"Good morning, Miss Jackson," Mr. Adewale says, turning into the Language hall as I enter right behind him.

As always, the bell for Spanish is about to ring above my head and I know Mr. Donald is going to have some shit to say if I'm late again. I don't have his favorite quarterback on my arm this morning because Nigel's off somewhere with Mickey. As long as I make it inside before the bell stops ringing, I should be cool with or without an escort.

"Good morning, Mr. Adewale. What brings you to South

Bay High this Monday morning?" I ask my favorite substitute teacher, speed-walking to my classroom at the far end of the long path. I don't want to rush off, but I have to. In an alternate reality me and Mr. A could sit down over coffee and chat about life and all of our experiences, but not now. If I were only a little older, I'd make him my man for sure.

"You know I can't stay away for too long," he teases as we approach my room. "Good game Sunday, wasn't it," he says, making small talk as he walks me to class. I feel so honored to be in his presence. It's not every day I get ushered through the halls by a fine teacher.

"Yes it was, especially because my boys won. It was an unexpected surprise to see you there," I say, giving him my biggest smile to date. I know he thinks that I'm just some corny teenager who has a crush on an older guy. But I'm actually interested in him on a whole other level, no matter how silly I may come across to him.

"I was a little surprised to see you yesterday too, given all the work you have on your plate for your research paper on Queen Califia, and the school play."

He looks at me curiously like he wants to ask me more questions, but stops himself just as his mouth forms the query. I guess he doesn't want to overstep his boundaries. I wish I could get it across to Mr. A just how open a book I am willing to be if he would only ask me what he wants to know. But it's like Ms. Toni said, the young brother will have enough drama just being at South Bay as it is. I don't want anyone to misconstrue our friendship as anything else. This isn't *Degrassi: The Next Generation* and my name ain't Paige.

"Yeah, well you know the boys need cheerleaders," I say, raising my hands in the air like I'm frantically waving two pom-poms.

Mr. A. laughs at my team spirit as he opens the heavy door, letting the cold air from the stark classroom hit us both in the face. Mr. Donald isn't at his desk and the bell's ringing, which means I could have been late without too much of a consequence, or so I think.

"Good morning class," Mr. Adewale says. "I'll be your substitute this week while Mr. Donald is at a coach's convention." He places his black leather computer bag on the near-empty desk before continuing. The class perks up at the announcement of having a sub all week. I know only about ten percent of the students will show up after today.

"What's up, Jayd," China says, speaking out of turn and pissing our sub off as I take my backpack off and set it on the floor. Mr. A gives China a look that sets the tone for the rest of the morning, I'm sure. As if she said nothing, Mr. Adewale continues with his announcement while unknowingly making my week.

"He's left me a lesson plan for the week and I made copies for each of you to take home. It's pretty self-explanatory, but if you have any questions just let me know." Mr. Adewale takes a stack of papers out of the back of his worn bag and passes me a few to hand out before I take my seat. I'm glad the new girl, Shawn, who now sits in the back of the room, got the message real quick that this was my seat without me having to say a word. I would like to know her story, but it'll have to wait for another day. Right now, I only have eyes for Mr. Adewale.

"Excuse me," China says from the back of the room. "I need to go see the nurse. I think I'm coming down with something." She feigns a cough as the rest of the class giggles. China's a trip and then some. Before Mr. Adewale can answer her request, another student interrupts, causing a slight commotion in the already animated room.

"Yeah, the munchies," her homeboy Doug says from his desk across the room.

Mr. Adewale's strong jawbone tightens, giving his chiseled face an even more attractive profile. Where is this man from?

"Shut up, Doug," China says, tossing a paper ball his way. They used to date last year but broke up over some stupid shit, like every other couple I know. Now they are the best of friends and, for the most part, inseparable.

"Okay, that's enough you two. Please start quietly on your assignments before I decide to add to your work," Mr. Adewale orders, silencing the dueling duo for now, and any other attempts to ditch class. The class settles down and we get to work.

"I didn't know you were a referee," I say, quietly striking up conversation with our sub. Luckily, my desk is close enough to his that he can hear me whisper. It's not coffee, but close enough to my dreams to make me smile. I plan on taking advantage of the remaining forty-eight minutes to get to know him a little better.

"And I didn't know you were dating Jeremy," he says, throwing me a curve ball way out of left field.

I wanted to give him the impression that my life was an open book, not a dartboard. What the hell?

"I'm not anymore. We're just friends now," I say, redirecting my attention away from his glistening hazel eyes and toward the board.

Where the hell did that come from? And why do I feel the need to justify myself to this brotha? I know he's all "Mr. Black Panther" or whoever, but damn, does he have to come at a little sistah so cold like that?

"I just took you for the type of young lady who wouldn't entertain the thought of dating a white boy, but I see I was wrong." Mr. Adewale smiles to let me know he's only teasing. but the depth of his voice tells me he's also slightly disap pointed. I recognize the tone from Rah's response when

first found out I was dating South Bay's most popular bache-
lor. He didn't get it then anymore than Mr. Adewale does
now.

"Well, my girl Nellie's dating Chance," I say, taking my
notebook and pen out of my bag to jot down the assignments listed on the board.

Mr. Adewale isn't going to make me feel guilty about my
shit. I don't have to explain my movements to him or anyone
else. Well, other than Mama and my mom, but never to a
dude—I don't care who he thinks he is.

"Birds of a feather flock together, right?"

He chuckles while looking through his looming stack of
work, only slightly amused by my humor before getting serious with me. Why is he acting like he knows me? "You are a
different kind of bird and we both know that."

Mr. Adewale knows something more that he's not letting
slip. I've always had the feeling that he knew me before we
met and I'm not second-guessing my intuition. I'll have to
ask Mama about getting information out of my new teacher
when I get home this afternoon. Until then, I'll enjoy the
back-and-forth we've got going on and the rest of my day.
Besides, why would I argue with him when what he says is
true? I am a different kind of bird and I'm ready to spread my
wings and let everyone see my true colors—Mr. Adewale included.

"How do you know anything about how I fly?" I ask. Mr. A
up straight in his seat, tapping his red pen against a stack
ms.

't know, but you could say I have a sixth sense about
s."

ura, Mr. A's got something else on his agenda
with me. I don't want to be caught off-guard
em. A hustler's always got to be one step
ition, and my advantage in this game is

Mama's wisdom. We'll see how deep his so-called sixth sense matches up against Mama's powers when I get home.

Instead of dealing with the impending drama between Mickey and Nellie, and apparently between me and Nellie too, I studied in the drama room at break, and my lunch was saved by our mandatory rehearsal. Laura worked my nerves to no end this afternoon. She keeps hinting that I'm going to be sorry, and soon. Usually I wouldn't take her threats too seriously, but something about her confident tone has me on edge today. If anything can calm my nerves it's Mama's cooking.

The scent of Mama's snickerdoodles carries me up the quiet block toward home. Mama's been stressed out with other people's issues at home and the homeless shelter alike. Baking always calms her nerves, and her sweet treats have the same effect on everyone who eats them. I can't wait to get my hands on a cookie.

"How was your day, baby?" Mama asks, as I enter the crowded kitchen, filled with Christmas decorations and specialty baking pans among other holiday crap Jay and I are responsible for handling. Every year we have to unpack all of the Christmas decorations and then put them up. It used to be fun being the youngest ones around here, but both of us have outgrown these duties. If my uncles acted right with their baby-mamas and stopped trying to be mac daddys, some of our younger cousins would be around to pick up the holiday slack.

Mama's dog, Lexi, shifts her slumbering body from one side to the other, allowing me space to sit at the kitchen table.

"It was cool. Other than the usual haters making my morning eventful, the rest of the day was smooth."

Mama stops kneading the cookie dough long enough to take a good look at me. Her green eyes look slightly red this evening, and I know immediately that she hasn't rested well or been taking her herbs. I'm too exhausted for an inquisition right now. Mama's lock is tight on me while she reads my face as I take my backpack off and put it on the floor next to Lexi. It must be nice being a dog and lying around all day.

"How was your day?"

Sensing my fatigue, Mama stops probing my mind for the time being and returns her energy to her baking. "Oh girl, you know the holidays are my busiest times and this year is no exception. Netta's going to help me out and I know you're still on board as one of my best helpers, right?"

I look at Mama and simply shake my head. Normally I'd sigh my disapproval, but tonight all I want to do is eat some cookies and go to bed.

"Right, Jayd?" Mama repeats her question, waiting for my answer. Now she knows something's up with me. "Okay, what's wrong? Did Rah, Jeremy, or both get on your nerves today?"

"Actually, it was Mr. Adewale and Nellie. They are both tripping hard and messing up my chi," I say, sounding more like a yogi than a descendant of voodoo priestesses.

Mama smiles at me while opening the hot oven to remove one large pan of her delicious treats before replacing it with another three dozen, ready to bake. The spirit room, Mama's private workshop, is good for small orders. But when she has to get down like this, the house kitchen is where it's at. She's been complaining about our old oven for years, but Mama's touch makes even this raggedy thing work magic.

"Chi, ashe; it's all the same thing," Mama says, reading my mind. I hate when she does that. "But why are they affecting it?"

"Well, Nellie's jealousy is getting worse and she's pimping Chance like he's a little puppy dog, and all I can do is watch.

And Mr. Adewale's up to something, but I don't know what it is."

Mama looks at me and starts humming a familiar song. I think she sang it to me in the womb. Sometimes Mama can trigger memories I had when I still wore my caul. As soon as I was born, it was violently destroyed by the ignorant nurses my mom had around her, but I still wear my veil like other children born like me.

"Jayd, you can't worry about what other people are up to. Haven't you learned that by now? You just have to keep yourself clean, and the best way to do that is to be up front and honest about all of your moves. Now, that doesn't mean going around and telling all of your business. It does mean that you don't lie about it though."

"But what if someone misinterprets your information—then what?"

Whatever Mr. Adewale knows about me has nothing to do with my life at school, that much I can tell. Still, I wonder what he's heard. Teachers gossip just as much as the students and I know Mrs. Bennett has given him an earful and then some about her favorite students to hate.

"You can't worry about how others are going to play their hand. You have to deal with the cards that have been dealt in front of you."

I love it when Mama starts talking like she's playing spades. That and bid wiz are her favorite card games, and she's good at them both, too. She and Netta used to play with Daddy and Netta's husband, back when Mama and Daddy acted like a couple. Now I'm usually her partner.

"That's the art of a true hustler, baby. It doesn't matter what tools you have in front of you. A true hustler will survive no matter if he has a paddle to get up shit creek or has to use his bare hands. Either way, he's going to make it."

"But this is different, Mama. There's more at stake than

losing a hand—or my pride. I can feel that whatever's up Laura's sleeve is big."

Mama passes me a paper towel with two piping-hot cookies inside. I can tell these will calm me down for sure just by their sweet scent. If Mama would sell her desserts and other treats for their true worth, we'd all be on easy street.

"Well, you need to call her bluff if you want to find out what's in her hand, baby girl."

Mama's right. Sometimes talking to her is like talking to an old player in the game. I guess that's her Legba side coming out, as she calls it.

"And as far as Nellie and Chance are concerned, that's their business. Whether you can see it or not, they are both getting something out of that relationship."

"But what can Chance possibly be getting, except for played?" I bite into the soft sugar cookie, licking the light sprinkles of cinnamon and sugar off my lips as I chew the fragrant treat. Damn, Mama's got skills.

"That's between Chance and Nellie. Just be sure it's a mutual situation between them. Everyone's out to hustle someone or something if they're being honest with themselves." Mama takes an angel-shaped cookie cutter out of the cupboard and covers it with flour before she cuts into the dough. The other shapes include Christmas trees, wreaths and snowmen. "When I first met Esmeralda I thought she was a godsend. Now I know better, but that lesson came after many years of what I thought was a true friendship."

"Yeah, but that's different than Nellie using Chance while she's still jocking Nigel. Not to mention the fact that in the meantime, she hates Mickey and can't stand me being friends with Chance. Now, how am I supposed to deal with that?" Maybe I should take a batch of cookies to my friends. We could all use some serious chilling out.

"Well, Jayd, you can only save yourself, and you'd better—

before your enemies take you down with them. I remember how happy I was to find Esmeralda and our former spiritual family. I thought I'd found my home. But after a few years working with them, I realized they drained people, took people's last dime, used their vulnerabilities as weaknesses to be exploited, not to mention other ways they took advantage of our clients. I realized quickly that they weren't really hustlers at all. They were the kind of people that hustled other people, and that's not a hustler—that's a pimp." Mama places the delicate angels on the parchment paper–covered sheet as she looks through the kitchen and across the living room toward Esmeralda's house. If she could blow Esmeralda up with her eyes, I'm sure Mama would have done so by now.

"Well I never thought I'd call Nellie a pimp, but she's one cane away from having her lean on point," I mutter in between bites.

Mama laughs at the thought of Nellie walking with a limp, but it's true. Nellie's got some kind of pimp potion working on Chance and I want some of my own to use for other reasons. Maybe there's a class I missed somewhere in junior high. All I know is Mickey and Nellie not only signed up for it, but could charge for tutorials.

"If you want to know about pimping, Netta's who you need to talk to. Ask her all about this tomorrow at the shop. In the meantime, go wash up and get ready to eat dinner. There's a plate of food waiting for you on my dresser," she says, opening the oven to check on the cookies. "You can eat in the spirit room while you study your lessons. I left your assignment on top of the spirit book."

Didn't Mama just hear how tired a sistah is? She looks at me as if to say she's tired too, and I know she is. But, as Mama also says, a woman's work is never done. I'll definitely ask Netta about the hustle tomorrow if I have the energy to remember. Right now, I'll gladly grub on my dinner and sneak a few more cookies after I'm done. I hope my lessons help me figure out what my next move is with Nellie, Mr. Adewale, and Laura, because I'm getting up this creek called high school with or without my paddle. If I have to crawl on my knees, I'm making it through Drama High, hating females, nosy teachers and all, because I've got something they don't have: a strong lineage mixed with some serious street knowledge.

~ 3 ~
Netta's Mojo

*"A new religion that'll bring ya to your knees/
Black velvet if you please."*

—ALANNAH MYLES

I'm so glad today is a short day. The only negative about it is that I didn't get to continue my conversation from yesterday with Mr. Adewale as I'd planned. I want to grill him more about what he thinks he knows about me. He seemed like he wanted to talk to me today as well, but Mrs. Bennett interrupted our Spanish class and took up his ear for the majority of the short period. By the time she was done yapping about nothing much, I'm sure, the bell was about to ring. I guess I'll have to wait until tomorrow to finish my inquisition.

Sometimes I wonder what we'd do without teachers' meetings. Short Tuesdays are what get me through the week, especially now that what little free time I have during the school day belongs to drama or AP. Even so, I'm going to take some time out today and *Google* Mr. Adewale again. I also need to catch up with Ms. Toni sooner than later. I've decided to take Mama's advice and one-up my competition by doing a little research of my own, but not before I catch up with my girls. I have to meet Mama at Netta's shop in a little while and I can't be late.

"Were you naughty or nice this year, Miss Jackson?" Mickey asks, teasing me with her Coach catalogue as we sit outside on the stadium bleachers. Mickey really gets into the holiday spirit when it comes to the receiving part. And this year if she plays her cards right she'll have two Santas checking her list.

"I'm always nice," I say, snatching the catalogue from her hand. She's got a stack of them ranging from clothes to jewelry and beyond. This girl's not joking about her Christmas list this year.

It's chilly outside, but I'm grateful to be out of rehearsal. With the heat on it's awfully stuffy and cramped in the drama room. I'll be glad when the Fall Festival is over and we can go back to our separate spaces. Having ASB share our class until the play is over is getting on everyone's nerves, especially Ms. Toni's. She's been unusually irritable—but still showing me some love, so it's all good.

"And what you about you?" Mickey looks across me at Nellie, who's still not really speaking to her. I guess she's embarrassed about her failed attempt to out Mickey to Nigel on Sunday. It's no use in hating Mickey, and I hope Nellie gets over herself soon.

"What about me what?" Nellie grabs a J Crew catalogue from the stack sitting on the bleacher below ours, and starts flipping through the pages. I'm surprised she didn't pick up the Tiffany catalogue, which has every-other corner turned in. I guess Mickey's dreaming real big this year.

"Naughty or nice," Mickey says.

I don't know if it's the pregnancy hormones or what, but Mickey's being unusually cool about Nellie trying to call her out. Maybe it's because Mickey knows she was wrong in the first place and doesn't want Nellie to stay mad at her. But Nellie's shoulder is colder than the sea breeze blowing across my cheek, and I don't see it warming up anytime soon.

"What difference does it make? There's no such thing as Santa Claus anyway." Nellie tosses the catalogue back in the pile and claims the Tiffany one for herself. She may not believe in Santa but I'm sure she still believes in getting gifts.

"Hush yourself," Mickey says, holding her stomach as if to cover the baby's ears. "You don't want Nickey Shantae to hear."

"Who the hell is that?" Nellie asks, shocked at Mickey's response.

Mickey used to be the main one cursing Santa out come the holidays. She always said her man was the real gift giver, so why front. Now that her maternal instincts have kicked in I guess Santa's real again.

"That's my daughter, fool." Mickey's a trip and Nellie ain't falling for it. "In my baby books they say that the baby's listening inside the womb and I don't want her childhood ruined by your sour ass."

"You already named the baby," I say, trading my catalogue for the Target brochure. I may dream a lot, but I try to keep my wish list in perspective. We are all struggling these days and I refuse to buy in to the holiday buzz. I'd rather my money be in my wallet any day than on my ass, as Mama would so eloquently put it.

"Yeah, and don't ask me how I know it's going to be a girl. I just have a feeling about it. Nigel swears he knows it's a boy."

Nellie looks at me and rolls her eyes at Mickey's family planning. But there's more to Nellie's disgust than just hating. I feel like she's plotting in that freshly-pressed head of hers, but I'm not sure what she's thinking.

"Do you have a name picked out for a son, just in case?" I ask.

Before Mickey can answer, Nellie smirks at my question as if the answer is obvious. "Of course she does. She probably picked it out when she first met Nigel." Nellie flips through the pale blue booklet without looking directly at her target.

"What's that supposed to mean?" Mickey demands reaching across my lap to snatch the catalogue away from Nellie's face, almost pushing me back across the bleachers behind us.

"Damn, Mickey, watch out," I say as she sits back down. I know that was a low blow on Nellie's part, but violence isn't the answer, especially not for an expecting mommy.

"It means just what it sounds like," Nellie says, straightening out the pages of her catalogue before continuing her browsing, and her conspiracy theory. "I think it's all very convenient, if you ask me."

"You think I planned this pregnancy?"

Mickey's as shocked as I am by Nellie's accusation. Ever since she was crowned Homecoming princess a couple of months ago, Nellie's become a lot bolder in the way she carries herself.

"You are a real trip, Nellie, you know that?" Mickey says.

"Whatever, Mickey. It doesn't even matter, right? You got the dude, locked him down in two months and can claim to be his baby-mama, maybe. You won. Now can we please talk about something else for a change?"

I don't like the tone of Nellie's voice. There's still too much hating in it for me.

"No we can't. Not until you let this go, Nellie," I interject before Mickey has a chance to respond.

Mickey looks at Nellie like she wants to rip right into her, but resists for her baby's sake. I look down at the bleachers below to see Misty, KJ, and the crowd laughing at our dramatic scene. We can get loud when we want to without being fully aware of just how big our mouths really are. If Mickey was still trying to keep her baby bump a secret, it's definitely out of the bag now.

"Jayd, how can I let it go when she keeps rubbing it in my face?" Nellie sounds like a wounded little sister whose big sis got the gift she wanted.

"No one's rubbing anything anywhere. It's a fact, Nellie.

We're going to be aunties no matter how you may feel about it, so you need to get over your jealousy and get with the program," I say, trying to lighten the mood. But with Misty glaring our way I don't think we're going to have much luck keeping the peace.

Mickey, back in shopping mode, breaks the momentary, uncomfortable silence, making Nellie's teeth grit even tighter.

It's going to be a long seven months.

"Jayd, what do you think of this baby crib? It converts from an infant to a toddler bed. And this crib converts all the way into a full bed, but I don't know if we want to keep the same baby bed for that long," Mickey says, pointing out the expensive baby beds to me in the Babies R Us catalogue she's studying like I do my government text. She's got every section tagged, with her favorites highlighted in fluorescent pink or powder blue. Some girls live to become doctors or models. Mickey's dream is to be a spoiled housewife, and it looks like hers is very close to coming true.

"I think it's too big to fit in your tiny-ass room that you share with your little sister. Where is she going to sleep?" Mickey's family is already bigger than Brad and Angelina's international brigade. How she thinks she and her lovechild are going to fit in that small house is over my head.

"Yeah, where are you and the baby going to live?" Nellie asks, turning her already sky-high nose up at a glowing Mickey. I'm glad she said it and not me, even if we are both thinking the same thing. "You already live with ten other people."

"Nigel's going to work that part out. My job is to decorate our home, and that's just what I'm doing, starting with the nursery. Kinda like your job is to hate and, by the way, you are excellent at it. Whoever haters like you report to should give your ass a raise." Mickey glares at Nellie, who looks like she wants to slap our girl across the face. But Nellie hasn't completely lost her mind.

"Yeah Nellie, what's up with you? Nigel ain't mad so why are you still tripping?" I ask, looking at Nigel from our spot in the middle of the bleachers. He runs across the field, turns counterclockwise and throws the ball downfield to his teammate, who catches the perfect pass.

Mickey stands up and cheers for Nigel, who promptly blows her a kiss before running back up the field. Misty and the rest of the South Central black crew took up the bottom bleachers, which is where Mickey prefers to sit and watch her boo play. I don't know if it's because she can see him better, or because she's farther away from the top of the stadium where her man tends to park when he comes looking for her. Either way, she's pissed about them sitting in our seats and decides to make her way down to say something.

"What's up, Mickey," KJ says, glaring at her through his Gucci shades. They're probably a gift from one of his college girls. He keeps at least one chick on the side no matter who he's dating at school.

"What's up is y'all are in our seats. You know this is where we chill." Mickey looks down on the crew, focusing on Misty.

"Yeah, I guess with your baby bump starting to show it's getting difficult to walk up the stairs, huh," Misty says, making Shae, Tony, and KJ and his boys laugh. But Mickey's not amused in the least. The last thing she wanted was Misty to get wind of her pregnancy, but Mickey might as well consider it news already spread.

"Yeah, my baby belly is making me a bit winded," Mickey says, rubbing her tiny bump. "But I guess it's difficult for you having to walk up the bleachers and clap at the same time." I knew Mickey was going to go there. I feel bad Misty contracted gonorrhea—another gift from one of KJ's broads that he decided to share with her—but I tried to tell Misty about KJ. Messing with him is like playing with fire, and she got burned, literally.

"Shut up, Mickey," Misty says, embarrassed. I know KJ was her first, and if she has anything to say about it he'll be her only. "If it means that much to you, take it." Misty gets up from her seat, ready to let Mickey take it, but Mickey's not done clowning my nemesis quite yet.

"You don't have any Lysol wipes or something you could use to disinfect the area after you get up? You should really think about carrying some sanitizer in your purse at the very least."

Now Mickey's gone too far. Even I feel bad for Misty, and from the looks of it, so does Nellie.

"Mickey, why do you think you can go around airing everyone else's dirty laundry except for your own? You're not so clean yourself," Nellie says, shocking us all.

"Oh, now this is good," Del says, turning completely around in his spot to witness the scene. "Nellie defending Misty against Mickey. Did hell freeze over or something?" KJ laughs and so does everyone else in their crew, excluding Misty, who looks like she doesn't know what to say.

"It *is* cold nigga. Maybe we should check the weather," C Money says, adding his two cents.

"C Money and Del, don't y'all have something better to do?" I say, walking down to join my girl, who can't decide who to go after now: Nellie or Misty.

"Hey, baby, my name is just Money now because I'm getting paid, you feel me," C Money says, claiming dap from his boys. I'm so glad I don't hang with these punks anymore.

"Well, whatever the hell your name is, mind your business." I escort my girl back to our seat, where Nellie is getting up. "And where are you going? We're not done." I grab hold of Nellie's arm as she heads down the bleachers. "Y'all need to handle this madness before it gets out of hand."

"It's already out of hand. I'm tired of feeling bad because you feel bad, Nellie. Grow the hell up," Mickey says, stuffing her pile of catalogues back into her bag before picking it up and storming down the bleachers to her chosen baby-daddy. "See you tomorrow, Jayd. Check your girl before I do." Nellie looks at her, and I can tell she's a bit shaken by the harshness of Mickey's words. Finally Nellie's waking up, or so I think.

"Mickey's got some nerve saying I need to be checked while she just runs around and does whatever the hell she wants to," Nellie says, rolling her eyes and neck. Mickey always has brought out the black in our girl.

"Whatever happened to Christmas spirit," KJ says as Mickey storms past them and onto the field where Nigel's taking a water break.

KJ thinks his shit is funny when it's not. We all choose to ignore his silly comment. What did I ever see in him?

"KJ, don't you have someone to infect?" I say, silencing him and forcing his boys to hold in their "oohs." I know that was low, but he pushed me. Like Nellie, sometimes KJ doesn't know when to shut the hell up.

"She's the one who needs to grow up. Trapping a dude with a baby is so outdated," Nellie continues, flipping her hair over her shoulder and now reminding me too much of Tania's trifling ass. How Jeremy ever went with Tania, and then me, I'll never understand. I'm just glad she's out of the picture. But unfortunately she still has a psychic hold on her followers.

Even after Tania tried to get Nellie to eat a worm-infested apple at the Halloween masquerade ball and Laura ended up taking the bait instead, Nellie and Laura both still hung out with Tania until she moved to New York, claiming it was only because of "official school business." Tania's got more power than Jim Jones when it comes to rich girl wannabes, Nellie included. It'll be interesting to see who rises to take her place.

"Well, you were okay with Tania's instant-wife-and-mother plan. What's wrong with Mickey doing it her way?" I pull my arms through my backpack and snap the straps across my stomach, ready for my trek home. Nellie will catch a ride with Chance, who's more than likely in the drama room chilling with Matt and Seth. Jeremy had to meet with his probation officer this afternoon, for the last time. I'm glad he got to stay at South Bay after he was caught selling weed at the beginning of the year and that they let him off so easily.

"The difference is, Tania never lied about her shit. She was honest and up-front, even if it did mean she had to move to New York and start a whole other life."

The way Nellie tells Tania's story makes me think of those shows on Lifetime about brides and their dream weddings. Nellie's deranged if she thinks Tania's living the life that ought to be lived. Has she forgotten it's Jeremy's baby this chick is passing off as her pure Persian heir, with her new husband in New York? Tania's family is just as racist as Jeremy's father when it comes to having a pure bloodline.

"Nellie, let me tell you something," I say to my friend as we walk up to the top of the bleachers so I can be closer to my bus stop. I have about five minutes until I need to get going. Mama's expecting me at Netta's and I have a lot of work to do today. They have me decorating the shop with all sorts of Christmas ornaments. The holidays feel more like slavery to me than a celebration. "Nigel's not getting hustled by Mickey. If anything, they're both getting exactly what they want out of their relationship. So why should we hate?"

"Because it ain't right," Nellie pouts.

Mickey's right; Nellie does need to grow up. She's letting her emotions get the best of her and that's not good for any of us. I wish I could convince her to come to Netta's with me and get a head cleansing to help her calm down, but I know that ain't happening no time soon. Nellie and Mickey both are still a bit leery of my lineage. If they knew the full extent of our powers they'd really freak out.

"Right or not, it's happening and we have to deal with it in the best way possible."

Nellie looks at me and I know she's not feeling my words. If I didn't know better I'd say her eyes were turning green with envy, and unlike Mickey's nonprescription contacts, green eyes don't look good on Nellie. I just hope she doesn't take her jealousy crusade too far, because I can only keep Mickey off of her for so long. After that, she's on her own.

"You deal with it your way, Jayd, and I'll deal with it mine." Nellie walks away from me, heading toward the drama room.

As the sun begins to fade in the distance and the slight warmth in the chilly air with it, I see our threesome slowly coming to an end. Mickey, Nellie, and I have been through a lot of shit in our two years hanging. We're opposites, but we've made it work this far. Leave it to a dude to mess up a good flow. I know Mama and Netta both will be able to shed some light on our situation and hopefully help me save our friendship before it's too late.

When I get to Netta's Never Nappy Beauty Shop the lights in the window are brighter than usual. Mama and Netta have already hung the outside lights, doubling the permanent strand of white lights that offset the bright neon pink sign in the front window. A red and green wreath is hanging over the peephole of the front door. I thought this was supposed to be my job, but I guess they couldn't wait to get started.

Netta buzzes the door, letting me in to their holiday fortress. "Hello little Miss Jayd, assistant extraordinaire," Netta says, waving her arms around, proud of their creation. It looks like Santa and his elves blew up in here. "How do you like it?"

"Well, you've definitely got spirit," I say, placing my backpack and jacket onto one of the three dryer chairs. I walk over to Mama, who is sitting in a chair, waiting for Netta to do her hair, and give her a kiss on the cheek. Then I head to the washbowl to wash my hands and face. Netta believes in doing a mini-cleansing before she begins her work every day.

"I take it from your tone you had a rough day," Mama says, picking up on my sentiments exactly. The last thing I want to do is hang up more Christmas decorations, especially when I have so much work to do. If being at the shop has to do with getting my hustle on, that's one thing. But more work with no pay doesn't attract me at all.

"Yeah. This madness between Mickey and Nellie has gotten out of hand," I say, taking my apron off the hook next to the washbowls. I'm ready to start my job, paid or not. Having an apprentice is the tightest hustle of all. I can't wait until I get to boss someone around.

"Now hold on there, young lady. People would pay top dollar for the kind of training you get being around Mama," my mom intervenes. It must be a slow day at work if she's all up in my head this afternoon.

"It is hella boring, but that's beside the point, Jayd. I don't like the vibe I'm getting from you right now. I know you had a bad day, but damn. Don't take it out on Mama or Netta. They can get funky right back, and trust me, their funk is more potent than yours will ever be."

"I know. It's just sometimes I feel like all I do is work. When do I get time to myself?" I know I'm whining, but it's true. Between school, work, family, and friends I rarely have a moment to clear my head.

"What else do you have to do, Jayd? Nothing; you're a teenager. If you have too much time on your hands, all you'll do is get in to some kind of trouble. That's why your friends are so twisted up now. Nellie and Mickey remind me of myself when I was a teenager. You need to be the voice of

reason, which means you can't get tired of working, girl.
You are a hustler, so get on your job and stop complaining,
you ungrateful child." And, with that mind-lashing, my mom
exits my thoughts before I have a chance to argue.

"Oh, this must be really good if your mother's in your head.
Tell me what happened," Mama says, picking up on my psychic beat-down. My mom's good for putting a sistah in check,
for real.

"Nellie just won't let up on Mickey being with Nigel and,
more importantly, with her not being sure if Nigel's the
daddy and the fact that he's okay with that." Mama looks up
at Netta's reflection in the mirror as she stands behind mama's
chair. Their eyes connect and they smile, realizing they are in
complete sync with their thoughts.

"Jayd, did I ever tell you about my lineage?" Netta clamps
the hot curlers three times, setting off a tone in the room. I
swear she just called a spirit in here: I can feel the tempera-
ture change in the room. When I was younger, they would
come often. Now, not so much, but I still know that chill
when I feel it.

"Not really. I just know your mother, sisters and grandmother all did hair." Netta smiles at the innocence of my
statement, ready to tell her story.

"Girl, when you're in someone's head you can make them
tell you anything you want to know. Anything," Netta says,
looking at Mama, who seems to be talking to her through her
facial expressions. No wonder they freaked my mom out.
"That's why this is a never nappy shop. When people leave
here, their heads are as clear as river water, I don't care the
texture of their hair. I do more than press and curls, you
know."

"Don't let your friends' drama cloud your judgment, Jayd.
You've got to keep a clear head always, and right now you're

too wrapped up in everyone else's stuff to focus on your own."

"You haven't even mentioned the play, and that's what I want to know about. Not more of your trifling friends. You done took my mojo, girl—look at your Mama's hair." Netta drops the hotcurlers back into their oven and spins Mama around to face me. Her hair is unusually flat, but it still doesn't look bad. "I've got to have good energy up in the shop to keep my magic, girl; that's my hustle. And, if you like money, you have to learn how to attract prosperity." She looks around the room and I know who she called in now: Legba, our father deity.

"Yes, Baba Legba is here, Jayd. Netta belongs to him, too." Mama gets up from her chair and leads me to the back, where Netta's shrine is housed. After checking the front door, Netta meets us in the back, ready to help a sistah clear her mind, I assume.

"Now Jayd, you have to come back here everyday before you start work, and leave your head at the door. No mess in my shop ever, you hear?" The shrine stands at least six feet tall, with all kinds of things on it for the various orishas. I can tell it's older than I am, and then some.

"Oh, Netta," I say, as she unveils the picture hanging behind the black velvet cloth. I always thought the cloth served as a backdrop for the shrine, which it does. But protecting the painting behind the curtain is its true purpose.

"Breathtaking, isn't she," Netta says, taking the thick cloth and tying a red ribbon around it. Golden bracelets pop out of the black velvet painting, leading my eyes up the amber arm of the woman kneeling by the river. Her head seems to merge into the water she's facing, but her reflection catches my eye.

"Did she just move?" I know I'm tripping, but I'll be

damned if she didn't just look at me through her mirror image in the water.

"I don't know. Did she?" Netta asks, causing Mama to giggle. Netta takes my hand and brings me closer to her station at the tall shrine. Mama stands behind us as Netta begins her ritual by pouring a libation to the four corners.

"We praise all of the orisha. We praise all of the ancestors. We praise Baba Legba and Mama Oshune. Jayd, you ring the bell while I light the candles." Netta passes the small brass instrument to me before taking the matches off the top of the five-tiered altar and lighting the yellow seven-day candle on the floor. This is how Mama's altar would look if she had the space.

"What makes you think the woman in the painting looked at you?" Mama asks, taking the bell from my hand and pushing me toward Netta.

"I don't know. It seemed like she was looking at herself in the water and then she looked at me." Netta turns around to look at Mama, who looks at me, and then they both look at the painting. Now I swear the painting is glowing. It may be all of the glittery paint on the velvet texture, but the woman and the water seem to glow.

"I know why Oshune is over mirrors," Netta chants. "I know why Oshune is over rivers. I know why Oshune is over rivers." Mama joins Netta in her chanting and I observe the lady at the river.

"Your friends are a reflection of you, just as you are of them. Remember that," Mama says, ringing the bell loudly as Netta continues the ritual. "And, like the river, you must look past its reflection to see what's on the other side. What do you think she sees in her reflection?" Mama points at the woman again, who is now looking past her reflection and through the water as if she's studying something only she can see.

"I don't know. The fish swimming?" I try to recall what's in a river. I don't remember the last time I've seen one up close.

"Yes, it can be that. Or it could be the gator about to rise up and snatch her off," Netta says. "We hairdressers have a unique power, and the mirror is the key to unlocking it. You're going to become a master by the time I'm done with you." Netta wraps her right arm around my shoulders, hugging me tightly as Mama rings the bell over my head. They are cleansing me: I can feel it, and the woman in the river is watching the entire scene through her reflection in the water and smiling coyly.

"There are many, many things that lie right beneath the surface, Jayd. If you're too busy looking at your own reflection you may not see the dangers that lie ahead." She's right about that. I have been wrapped up in everyone else's madness and not focused fully on my own shit.

"That's why it's so important not to let just anyone touch your head, child. There's all kinds of mojo in our art." Netta releases her hold on me, grabs a large pink notebook from the bottom of her shrine, and opens it. This must be her family's spirit book. She opens it to a page that has a drawing of a lady, with long hair on one side of her head and a shaved head on the other.

"What happened to her?" I ask, watching Netta pass the book from me to Mama, who laughs at the sight.

"Oh, I remember that," Mama reminisces. "She learned not to mess with us, now didn't she? Never piss off your cook or your hairdresser, Jayd. Remember that."

"Girl, your Mama showed that uptight wench who was the real queen that day. Here, read for yourself, Jayd. These lessons are now yours to absorb, too."

Oh great, more work. See what I'm saying?

Mama looks at me as if she heard my thoughts and I know

I'm in for it now. "You must listen to Netta and follow all of her directions, Jayd. No sassing ever, you hear," she says.

Netta flips through the pages—there must be at least five hundred or more.

"Yes ma'am," I answer. Netta points me back out of the small room and back into the salon where she and Mama resume their hair session.

"Now Jayd, working here is no easy task and I know you've got a lot on your plate, but I also know that you can handle it, starting Friday. I have regulars on the weekends that are very particular, but you'll learn. Also, never let anyone back to the shrine, or let them see the spirit book. Certain things are for our eyes only."

"And all of the clients don't know 'bout her powers or that she is still my best friend, so keep your mouth shut and be careful of what you hear."

I know how they get to talking in the beauty shop. That's why Mama has her very own day reserved.

"We've always had the touch, Jayd, that's no secret. But keeping it is. Using other people's thoughts against them is not only wrong, it's as close to a sin as I believe there is. That's how people get tricked and used, basically become zombies for others to use up. We never want to drain people, Jayd, especially not those we love. That's not how we get what we want."

I remember how scared Trish looked when she found out I was still braiding Rah's hair. I wonder—if I concentrated hard enough, could I get inside of his head?

Reading my devious expression, Netta scolds me with her eyes. "We fortify the mind, not strip it. Use your powers for good, little queen. You'll learn soon enough how to get everything you want, and more, without scheming. Remember that and you'll do just fine." Netta curls a perfect bump onto Mama's crown. I guess my cleansing worked for her, because she's definitely got her mojo back now. "Now, finish reading about the lady with half a crown, and after you're done with that, please finish putting the finishing touches on the decorations and sweep the floor."

Working with Netta's going to be a lesson all its own, and with Mama right here I'm sure I'll get the lessons of a lifetime. I'm just glad to be here and close to home for a change, even if it does mean more work for me. That's just how the hustle goes sometimes, I guess. And we hood folks know all about getting our hustle on.

~ 4 ~
Straight Outta Compton

"Niggaz start to mumble, they wanna rumble/
Mix em and cook em in a pot like gumbo."

—N.W.A.

I didn't get a chance to talk to Mickey or Nellie at all because of my AP meetings all day yesterday. Now that they're not talking again, it's going to be difficult hanging out. I thought after the game this past weekend everyone would resume chill status, but I was so wrong. Rah has been busier than ever, trying to get as much paper as he can in his hands before the holidays and before his court date. He's got a good lawyer, but she's not free. I miss Rah when he's not around, but I understand all too well about getting your hustle on.

Speaking of hustling, Mickey's ain't so tight these days. All of her drama is seeping into other people's lives, including mine, and my school friends are already too close to home as it is. I was always uncomfortable with the fact that we all live in the same hood and go to a white school outside of Compton. The other students got in on an out-of-district voucher program at our local high school, but my mom applied for it too late and had to use a friend's address to get me into South Bay. It's a volatile mix, mainly because the hating doesn't stop. There are only a few black students at the entire school, making it easy to spread news quickly no matter where we are.

And now with my girls hating each other, it's going to be

even more uncomfortable around Nellie, Mickey, and their men. Part of me wants to take sides, but I can't. I'm the only one thinking clearly. Between Mickey's pregnancy hormones and Nellie's jealousy, I don't know what's going to happen next.

"What's taking you so long in there, princess? Other people have places to be too," Bryan says, interrupting my morning bathroom time. He's got some nerve rushing me, considering how long it takes his primping behind when he gets in here.

"Now I know you're not talking. If I didn't know how you look, I'd say you were a pretty boy judging from how long you're up in this mirror." There are only three mirrors in this house: the one in the bathroom, the one above the dining room table, and the one in Mama's room. None of them are full length, but I usually stand on top of the clothes hamper in here to get a full view of my outfits.

I gather all of my toiletries, pajamas, and purse, ready to clear out anyway. Today is the first dress rehearsal for *Macbeth*, and I want to get to school on time to try to catch Mrs. Sinclair in the drama room. I'm anxious to see my costume, and want to lay my hands on it before Laura gets her clutches in the mix. I want to make sure my ashe is all over that dress.

"Shut your jaw jacking and hurry the hell up. I got to get on the corner before I get to work," Bryan says.

"When are you going to get a legal hustle and give up your non-job on the corner?" I ask. One more look in the mirror and I'll let him in. Whoever said beauty couldn't be rushed obviously didn't live in a house full of dudes.

"It is legal, baby girl. I know what you're thinking, but I'm not talking about that. Besides, when did I ever need to stand on the corner to slang a dime bag?" He and Rah have had the same side hustle for as long as I can remember. The shame is that Rah's game is much tighter than Bryan's when it comes to slanging herb. But it still doesn't make it right, and it isn't a good choice for either one of them. "And why you all up in my grill this morning? Get out now, Jayd. I gotta go."

"Whatever, punk," I say, opening the door slightly and taking my time just to piss him off.

"Haven't you heard of respecting your elders?" Bryan is more like my older brother than my uncle. How can he expect me to take him seriously?

"Haven't you heard of acting your age and not your shoe size?" I push him out of the doorway to make my way back into the room he and Jay share with Daddy. I place my things back into one of the three Hefty garbage bags I use to hold my stuff in the room's smallest closet and close the door.

"Whatever, smart-ass," Bryan says, stepping into the bathroom and laying his things down on the hamper.

I step into the hallway, ready to grab a banana from the kitchen and head out the door. I pull the bathroom door shut, pissing Bryan off even more.

"I just know you better start showing a little respect around here, that's all I'm saying," he says, reopening the door so I can hear him clearly. "By the way, my girl likes my braids," he says, rubbing his hands across the cornrows still tight under his do-rag. "When can I get a touch up?"

"I don't know, maybe tonight." I'm already exhausted enough as it is, and I have a lot of work on my plate. "I start working at Netta's tomorrow after school and then Rah's taking me to my mom's for the weekend."

"What's up with your mom? How come lil Lynn never has us over? She acts like she ain't my sis no more."

I live with four of my mom's six brothers and truth be told, I don't think of her as their sister either. My mom only comes over on Christmas Eve and Mother's Day, just like everyone else who wants to stay on Mama's good side.

"I have a feeling she'll be coming over here before she'll invite anyone over her house. You know my mom likes her privacy."

"And her men," Bryan says, sounding like my dad, but I know Bryan doesn't have any venom behind his words.

"Just one man, and he's cool—a real gentleman. You could learn a thing or two from him." Speaking of which, my mom better get over here soon for her reading or Mama will find a way to my mom's house in Inglewood.

"Whatever. If he ain't big pimping, that nigga can't teach me shit. I got my swagger tight, you feel me, girl?"

What is it with dudes and their swaggers? If I hear one more brotha talk about their pimp stroll or gangster lean, I'm going to scream.

"No, I don't." I gather my backpack and jacket from the dining room table, ready for my morning walk to the bus stop. Leaving through the back door is inconvenient because I have to fight my way out the back gate, which has been broken ever since I can remember. But it beats having to look into Esmeralda's evil eyes any day.

"I know you feel me Jayd. I can respect your frontin', even if there's no future in it. Don't forget about me tonight, Jayd. And maybe I'll even come by the shop and give you some work. All it takes is one steady client to get the ball rolling." Bryan turns on the faucet to get the hot water running. It takes a minute for the hot water heater to warm up.

"That'll be cool, if Netta lets me. Right now, I'm strictly the helper—but we'll see, since you're family and all." I can remember from my mom's own spirit journal entries that Netta doesn't like traffic in her shop, unlike other salons I know of. Mickey had an incident in her old salon and couldn't go back because of all the drama she and her man created there one day. I already know Netta's not having nothing like that in her space.

"Bet, Jayd. Now get on before I'm late for the van. My boy Carlos got a sweet deal on Christmas baskets and them ugly-ass Cabbage Patch Kid dolls. We're going to sell them in the back of the alley behind Miracle Market. You should come and check us out. You might see something you like." Knock-off Cabbage Patch Kid dolls and Christmas baskets out the back of a van. That's the best hustle I've seen since my Uncle Junior, the oldest of Mama and Daddy's children who also lives in the den with two other uncles, was selling DSL routers and tube socks in the same spot last year.

These brothas around here always got something going. That's why I love my hood. I can find everything I need within walking distance if I'm not too picky or particular about where it came from. So what if the router's not in a box and the socks are two sizes too big? If it works, I'm happy to stay ignorant about the origin.

"I'll check y'all out after school. Maybe I can pick up something for Mickey's baby." It'll be nice to have a baby to shop for again. Ever since my little cousin Nailah was born eight years ago, there hasn't been another baby girl around to pamper. My mom, Mama, and I all love to shower little girls with gifts. If Rah's daughter were around more, I'd probably do the same thing for her. And with the way Rah's concentrating on fighting for sole custody of his daughter, I better get my cash straight because I have a feeling I'll be seeing her soon.

"Mickey still trying to figure out who the daddy is?" I see Bryan's caught up on the neighborhood gossip. This city's too small to keep hot news quiet for long.

"I think she's already settled on that one."

Bryan gives me a look of recognition. I know he's been

down the maybe-baby-daddy path before and he knows better than to run around without covering up now.

"Well, she'd better make sure. Everyone knows how crazy
her man is. It's only a matter of time before he gets wind of
her creeping." Bryan takes his toiletries out of their Ziploc
bag and arranges them neatly on the bathroom sink. The
steam coats the bag, making it appear cloudy, just like my
mind is when it comes to the drama between my girls.

"Yeah, Mickey's on Nigel's jock hard. I hope she tells her
man soon. Maybe her truth won't be so catastrophic if she
tells him herself. But they're not hiding a thing. Mickey was
Nigel's biggest cheerleader at the game last weekend and
kicks it with him all of the time."

"Ah yeah, I heard Rah and them kicked KJ's ass on the
court last weekend. I never thought I'd see the day KJ lost a
game of one-on-one. But if anyone could do it, it would be
your boy, Rah. I really think he missed his calling," Bryan
says. Little does he know that Rah's missed a lot of things
lately. "I hope KJ's ego isn't bruised too badly."

"Now you and I both know KJ's head needed deflating.
I'm just glad I was there to witness it." And, with Mr. Adewale
and Jeremy there, I was really in heaven that day. Too bad
Misty, Sandy, and Trish showed up. But even they couldn't
burst my bubble.

"Yeah, but you know that a nigga with a bruised ego is the
most dangerous nigga out there. You tell Mickey to remember that shit when she breaks the news to her man. I'll holla
at you tonight."

As Bryan tends to his morning ritual, I begin my trek
through the kitchen and out the back door. Lexi's lounging
in her usual spot at the bottom of the back porch steps, chewing on a bone she dug up from only she knows where.

"Bryan's got a good point, huh girl," I say to Mama's dog
before unlocking the dilapidated gate. If we don't latch both

locks on the back of the wooden gate, both of the doors will swing open all day long. Last time I left the gate open, Lexi ended up pregnant. Mama finally got her spayed last year, but that was after she'd given birth to four litters. Mama says even Lexi's affected by Oshune's fertile powers. Lexi looks up at me, making sure I lock the gate before returning to her bone. Must be nice to live pretty much drama-free. Too bad we all can't live in a canine's reality.

By the time I got to school, it was too late for me to run down to the drama room to try on my dress. I guess I'll have to wait until lunch like everyone else. It's already break and I'm itching to see my costume but, as usual, Mrs. Sinclair's nowhere to be found. She lives around the corner and goes home to visit her babies any time she can, break included. I don't know how she keeps up her busy schedule, but she does it like a pro. I know her ex-husband, Mr. Sinclair, hates hearing from his students—Chance and Jeremy included— about how happy she is. But that's what he gets for cheating on her and treating her like crap when they were married.

I need to build with Mickey about how she's going to deal with her man and Nigel, but that conversation will have to wait until another time. I didn't feel like dealing with either of my girls today, so I'm going to spend the rest of my time in the library digging up more information on Queen Califia via Mr. Adewale's college paper. I tried to catch up with Ms. Toni, but she was out of her office. She's been busy with the drama festival and her regular duties as ASB advisor. But we have to talk soon. I have a lot to catch up with her about. I haven't talked to her about Mickey or Rah in a while and I could use some of her wisdom.

"Please check your bag at the front desk," the ancient librarian says to me as I pass by her station.

"Since when do we have to leave our backpacks?" I notice

the new set of cabinets behind the librarian's counter. There are only a handful of students present and all of the computers are available, so I should be able to get done pretty quickly. I just want to print out whatever I can find on the web. I'll finish my research and bibliography before the week is out. Our papers are due the last week of school, and that's only two weeks away. Time sure does fly when I'm procrastinating.

"Since my books, magazines, and other things are starting to come up missing."

The way she looks at me tells me she thinks I might be one of the kleptomaniacs. As much as I'm in here, I could jack her ass, but that ain't how I roll.

"Please take a number and leave your bag in the corresponding cubby. You can take your books out and take them with you while you work, if need be."

Ain't this some shit? I'm already down to the last ten minutes and I don't want to waste anymore time.

I take a seat at the computer closest to the cubby where my bag is. If there are kleptos on the loose, I don't want them getting my stuff either, especially not my charm bags and other spiritual items. Not that anyone would know what to do with them. But just the thought of someone touching my personal items bugs the hell out of me.

I take Mr. Adewale's card out of my purse and type in the web address listed for his graduate school. He must be hella smart to get a master's degree from the University of West LA. I hear they have a rigorous academic program. When his page pops up, a list of every publication he's written appears on the side of the page.

Fine and talented—just how I like my men, I think to myself as I search his page. The Califia paper is second to last in the long list of titles. I'll just print this out and read it later. Before I open the twenty-five page document, I notice the title "Voodoo Vixens" among the forty-plus documents and click on it.

"What the hell?" I scroll the document quickly, recognizing some of the names from our spirit book at home, Maman Marie's name included. "What does he know about my lineage and why is he calling my great-grandmother a vixen?" Now I'm going to have to break out five dollars to print both documents, but I have a feeling it'll be worth it.

"There's the warning bell," the librarian says, her shrill voice slicing the quiet air. "Please don't forget to claim your bags before exiting the building." The printer releases the pages on her side of the counter. Noticing the content of my papers, her eyebrows rise and she looks a few shades whiter than she did when I walked in. I wonder if campus gossip reaches the ears of the librarian too?

"How much do I owe you?" I ask, taking my wallet out of my Lucky purse and giving her my number for my bag's freedom. She looks at me like she's afraid to speak and turns around to gather my backpack and print outs.

"It'll be five dollars, young lady." Instead of handing me my items, she places them on the counter in front of me. Now, any other time she would have given it directly to me, but I guess she's afraid to touch me now. And that's just fine with me. Mama doesn't like too many folks touching us anyway. She says everyone's ashe isn't so easy to wash off.

"Thank you." I pass her the cash and retrieve my bag and papers from the counter. I can't wait to read all of this info and grill Mr. A about it the first chance I get.

Before I reach the main hall to cut through the senior quad toward government class, I notice Mr. A walking in the same direction from the main office. It's nice seeing him around campus so regularly, especially since Ms. Toni's so busy lately. I also think she's still disappointed in me for dating Jeremy, but what can I say? There's definitely something about Jeremy's swagger that moves me. Bryan could learn a thing or two from Jeremy about how to treat a girl.

"Good morning, Miss Jackson," Mr. Adewale says, falling into step with me, both of us quickening our pace to beat the bell.

"Good morning, Mr. Adewale. Or should I say, Mr. Voodoo Vixen Investigator extraordinaire."

Noticing my sarcasm, Mr. A stops in his tracks and looks down at me, his hazel eyes shimmering in the hazy sunlight. It was cloudy a little while ago, but the late-morning sun is melting away the gloom, giving Mr. Adewale a healthy glow.

"I see you've finally gotten around to doing your research. So, tell me what you found out." Mr. Adewale opens the classroom door, letting me in. Jeremy's already seated in his usual chair right next to mine. He looks up from his text book, catching my eye. But I really need to talk to Mr. Adewale. I nod "what's up" and refocus my attention on our substitute teacher.

"Well, I found out that you know more than you're saying about a lot of things, my lineage included." I sit down in the chair next to the teacher's desk and open my backpack to reveal his writings. "I haven't read them all, but what's this voodoo vixen paper all about?"

"Good morning, class," Mr. Adewale says, momentarily ignoring me while quieting the buzzing class. "Today you are to work on your research papers, which are due the week after next. Also, you need to reread chapter fourteen for your quiz tomorrow morning. You can talk quietly if need be, and I'm here if you have any questions."

"I have a question on the floor that's still unanswered," I quietly remind him, as Mr. A makes himself comfortable in Mrs. Peterson's chair. I can't wait until she's retired and he's here full time. It'll be nice to have another teacher I can look up to for a change.

"Yes, you do," he says, taking off his thin-rimmed silver glasses and placing them on the stack of papers on the desk in front of him. "Weren't you supposed to be looking up Califia?" He looks me in the eye and I can tell he's trying to read my expression, but I'm not that easy.

"I did. I printed that out, too. But this caught my eye. I couldn't resist." I toss the heavy report down on top of the paper pile and await his response. His golden brown cheeks flush with embarrassment, but from what, I wonder. "You can't be that surprised that I found this interesting, can you?"

"No, not at all. I just hoped you wouldn't find it just yet. I wanted to take more time before talking with you about it."

"Well, what's there to talk about?"

Mr. A looks at me, then out toward the rest of the class. He looks like he wants to tell me a big secret and I think it's bigger than I can imagine. What the hell is really going on with this brother?

"Jayd, there's more than meets the eye, don't you agree?" He looks at me, his hazel eyes sparkling with no help from the sun this time.

What's Mr. A not telling me about his knowledge of my lineage?

"Yes, I do. Which is why I'm asking you what you have against voodoo queens. Why do they have to be vixens?"

Mr. A picks up the familiar text, flipping through the pages and quickly skimming the words. He chuckles as he reads more, making me wait patiently for his response.

I glance across the room at Jeremy, who's waiting for me to come and sit down. I want to catch up with him too, but I never know for sure when I'll get to see Mr. Adewale again, so Jeremy will have to wait until lunch. He sent me a text this morning when he didn't see me at the bus stop and I told him he could come with me to the dress rehearsal since it'll be more laid-back than a normal rehearsal.

"Do you know the meaning of the word vixen, Jayd?" Mr. A looks at me.

"Is this a trick question? I know it's a negative word for a female, or else that book about the video chick wouldn't have sold so well."

Mr. A laughs at my reasoning. "Yes, Jayd, that is true. And that's why I titled the term paper what I did. But a vixen is actually a female fox. They're survivors, Jayd, true hustlers, if you will. This paper was a praise for the queens. But, like everything you sell, the packaging is what gets it a first glance, and an A in this case."

"Okay, you worked your way around that one. But what was all that about me being a different bird last time we talked? What do you know about my lineage?"

Mr. Adewale looks past me towards Jeremy and then back at me. His chiseled jawbone tightens. Now I know I've hit a nerve.

"Jayd, I know a lot more than you think. What I don't know is why you aren't more open about who you really are. I'm originally from Compton, also by way of New Orleans. I know who your grandmother is and, more importantly, who your great-grandmother was, and her history with white men. Haven't you learned anything from your history?"

Damn, not another hater. "I know you think you know me, but you don't."

"Jayd, you asked me, I didn't come at you. I didn't want you to feel self-conscious around me. But you have to admit it's a mighty small world."

Yeah, too small if you ask me.

"Please don't be defensive," he adds.

"I've got to get to my work. Thanks for the info." Mr. Adewale lets me rise without protest, even if his eyes are screaming for me to stay.

"What was that all about?" Jeremy asks, looking up from his book and pulling my chair out for me to sit down.

How do I begin to tell Jeremy about my lineage and the fact that there are research papers online that include my ancestors and grandmother's name?

"History, what else?"

Jeremy wouldn't understand if I told him. Besides, we have our own fish to fry, as Mama would say. I haven't talked to Jeremy since he made the comment about always being here for me. I know he wants to explore more of an open relationship with me again, but I'm not ready for all that. Besides, Mr. A is right about me not being all that comfortable dating a white boy, even if it is Jeremy. Why do things always have to be so complicated with him?

"Well, it's nice to see you this morning. I missed you at the bus stop again, but it's cool. I can't wait to see you in your costume at lunch. I know you're going to look hot in it no matter what it looks like."

Jeremy looks a bit hurt by my independence, but that's on him too. He should've never let me get used to walking to the bus by myself again.

"Yeah, I was too late to see it earlier. I hope Laura doesn't get her claws on my dress before I do." I've been keeping my distance from the broad since Monday's loaded exchange. Jeremy chuckles at my hate for his enemy's girl. At least we have our haters in common.

"By the way, what's up with your girl Mickey? I heard something about her having Nigel's baby."

Where's he been? News travels slowly when you're catching waves all day, I guess.

"Yeah, it's a bit uncomfortable in my camp these days, to say the least."

I know he can feel me on the tension between my girls. When Tania was here and I found out she was carrying his lust child, our time together was very uncomfortable. Retrieving my textbook from my backpack, I glance out of the open door to see Misty walking by. Her ass always finds a way to get out of class. Instead of ignoring me like she should, she smiles wickedly at me. She only looks me in the eye when she's got something up her sleeve that she knows will get under my skin. What's she up to now? Whatever. I don't have time to waste thinking about her and her madness.

"Is Mickey keeping it?"

I look up from my textbook, shocked at his question. We really do think differently.

"Of course she is. Why would you ask that?" I try to whisper, but my voice carries my discontent across the room. Mr. Adewale looks at me and places his index finger over his lips, signaling me to tone it down.

"I mean, she was messing around with Nigel as well as her boyfriend, right? I just figured she didn't know who the father was for sure."

"She doesn't, but that's not the baby's fault. She still deserves to be born."

Jeremy looks up from his work and smiles at me, but not in a charming way. It's that paternalistic grin he gets when he thinks I'm being too simple about something.

"Yes, that's true. But does the baby deserve to be born into a situation that's unhealthy for both the child and parents?"

I hate to admit it, but he does have a good point. Yet and still, that's no reason to jump to conclusions.

"Did you feel the same way when Tania told you she was pregnant?"

Without missing a beat, Jeremy answers assuredly, much to my disappointment.

"Yes, of course I did. I just assumed everyone considers abortion as an option."

My eyes begin tearing as I further realize how polar opposite our values are. "Well, you know what they say about assuming things: it makes an ass out of you and me. Well, actually this time it's just you, but you get what I'm saying."

Looking slightly hurt by my sass, Jeremy carefully considers his next move. "Jayd, you can't be serious. If more people would exercise that option, there wouldn't be so many poor children in the world."

"That's the same reasoning elitists use for welfare. If that's the case, me and the vast majority of people in my hood wouldn't be born."

Jeremy seems completely unconvinced by my argument. Frustrated, I glance over at Mr. A, who can hear every word of our discussion, looking for a little support. He looks up from his papers and gives me a look as if to say, "I told you so" and then returns to his work.

What the hell?

"Jayd, I'm not saying that children shouldn't be born. Of course they should be. The people that have them just need to consider all of their options and the baby's well-being before adding to an already full load that life brings with it. That's all I'm saying."

Jeremy really doesn't hear the stupidity in his words, but I do and it's making my blood boil. The last thing I want to do is get into a full-on argument with him when we are just getting back to a space where we can be friends.

"Babies aren't a burden to everyone," I say, burying my head in my studies and ceasing our conversation for the time being. Every time I forget we're from different hoods, Jeremy says something to make me remember. Right now I'm going to concentrate on my schoolwork and try to forget about everything else. I'll talk to Mama about Mr. Adewale's research when I get home.

*   *   *

After my discussions with Jeremy and Mr. A today I just wanted to chill for the remainder of the afternoon. They both gave me a lot to think about and I wasn't prepared for either conversation. Looking around my neighborhood, I see many children outside playing and yes, most of them come from single-parent households. And yes, some don't know their daddies, but they still seem happy enough. The more I think about Mr. Adewale's rationale for calling my ancestors vixens, the more I understand it.

"Jayd, where's your Mama at?" Pam, the neighborhood crackhead, whispers like she's on a top secret mission.

I just left Bryan's post outside of Miracle Market where he's getting his side hustle on. She was there begging for money or the opportunity to make it, as usual. Her pregnant belly is growing bigger, even if the rest of her seems to be dwindling away. Now I could see why someone would suggest she get an abortion. But like Mama says, you never know which ancestor you're keeping from coming back when you kill the unborn.

"I guess she's at the house, Pam. Why don't you go see for yourself?" Before I can finish my sentence, Pam walks off back toward the market. I feel for that girl in a real way. Bryan went to high school with her and said she was fine back in the day, but that's not the Pam I know.

Continuing my walk home, I can feel someone's eyes on me but I don't see anyone else around. I hope Esmeralda's not trying to focus her evil eyes on me again. I'm in no mood to fight her off. Before I can check my paranoia, Mickey's man rolls up in his black-on-black Monte Carlo with his personalized GANSGTA plates. Why is this fool following me?

"What's up, little witch girl?" Mickey's man says, rolling down his tinted windows, revealing his beet-red eyes.

Is he ever sober? "Nothing." The last thing I want to do is engage him in conversation. I haven't forgotten his indecent proposal the last time I saw him at Mickey's house. That may be the way they get down, but I'm cool with sleeping on my enemy.

"Why are you in such a hurry? You should come take a ride with me. We have some catching up to do." He abruptly turns the corner in front of me and pulls into an empty driveway, blocking my path.

"I have to get home." I step around his car, but not before he can open the heavy door, blocking my exit even more. What does he want with me?

"Not so fast."

Brandy's little brother, Tre, rolls down the passenger-side window. I knew he was hanging with some gangsters, but I was hoping he'd stay away from this crew. They are nothing but trouble and he just got out of jail. The last thing he needs is another strike against him.

"Word on the street is that my girl's been messing around and that you hooked them up. And I trusted you," Mickey's man says, chewing on the raggedy toothpick in his mouth.

"What the hell," I say, for lack of a better expression. "Why would I hook up Mickey with anyone when I know she's with you?"

"I don't know why bitches do any of the shit they do. Maybe because you want me all to yourself. I know where you're from, Miss Nutty Block. You want a gangster to show you the ropes."

"As if, fool," I say, passing him by. "If you know where I'm from, then you know who my uncles are and who my grand-mother is, so back the hell off." Amused by my heat, he gets out of the car and steps close to me, snatching my right arm.

"I like it when you're mad." He pulls me closer to him, his beer-ridden breath hot on my face.

What does Mickey see in this punk?

"Hey man, you need to step off my niece before I bust this cap in your ass, nigga," my uncle Bryan says, running around the corner to my rescue. I'm glad he did, because for a split second I almost lost it.

"I was just talking to her, man. No harm." Mickey's man lets go of me and gets back in his car, blaring N.W.A. loudly before stating his final warning. "You make sure you tell that nigga I'm coming for him, you hear?"

Bryan stands beside me, putting his piece back in his pants. "Jayd, you okay?"

This is one of those days I wish Rah was here.

"Yeah, I'm cool." I feel like I've just been raped. Mickey better handle her shit before I'm forced to take matters into my own hands.

"Jayd, I don't know what Mickey's gotten you into, but you better check your girl. That was a bit too close for me."

"Don't worry, I will." Mickey's going to get more than a piece of my mind come tomorrow. I'm with Nellie now; this shit has gone way too far.

"Does Rah know what's going on with Mickey's man? You know he deals with them niggas, too."

"No, I didn't know that." This city is too damned small for me. If Mickey's man knows Rah, it's only a matter of time before he finds out about Nigel. Thank god Nigel doesn't live in Compton anymore. But location will only buy him a little time. True retaliation knows no boundaries and that's the only way Mickey's man and his crew roll. They are straight out of Compton, for real.

"Well, you might want to holla at your boy about your girl and her man. This shit is getting serious, Jayd, and you may be in over your head."

Bryan's right. I need to let Rah help with this one. But before I see him tomorrow, I need to warn Mickey about her man and me, because I'm not taking on her bad decisions any more. Her mess has brought too many people down and it's time one of us stepped up to the plate.

~ 5 ~
It's On

"Mama said knock you out/
I'm gonna knock you out."

—LL COOL J

"*I* never read anything about Lady Macbeth having a weave," Laura says. She and the usual haters stand around me while I apply my makeup in the dressing-room mirror. I have on an orange robe and my hair is pulled back in a red, black and green bandana. It's opening night and the dressing room is crowded with cast members, groupies, and parents. Everyone's parents except for mine.

"Me neither. I guess that's why you didn't get the part," I say, rolling my eyes at her in the mirror and continuing to get dressed. For some reason, even in my dream, I haven't seen my costume yet.

"Touché, Jayd. Touché," Laura says, stepping closer to my chair while Reid checks his makeup in the wide mirror. Without notice, Laura runs her manicured fingertips through my hair, sending a wave of panic through my head.

"What the hell's the matter with you? Get your hands off me," I scream at her, silencing the buzzing room.

Mrs. Sinclair and Mrs. Bennett run into the dressing room to see what all of the commotion's about. Before I can explain, Laura accuses me of attacking her and everyone in the room is silent.

"You little liar. I did no such thing. You came at me," I

say, proclaiming my innocence. But I'm in a room full of people who don't support me, except for Mrs. Sinclair, who looks perplexed. But I get the feeling the final decision's not hers to make.

"Come now, Jayd," Mrs. Bennett says. "We all know your tendencies and they're anything but passive."

Entering the scene late, Jeremy's mom catches up with another parent and heads over to add her two cents. I knew she was a member of the drama department's booster club because her name was on the stationery, but I thought she was more of a financial contributor than an active participant. Mrs. Sinclair looks from Mrs. Bennett to Laura to me. As she holds my costume, her eyes sadden and I know I've lost her vote.

"As a senior member of the booster club, I vote that we let the understudy fill in as Lady Macbeth until this matter is resolved," Mrs. Weiner says, adding her venom to the mix.

"But there are only three shows in the two-day festival. I can't afford to be on trial," I say, mocking the impromptu judge and jury session. How did Laura touching my hair escalate into this big mess?

"Didn't I tell you not to let anyone touch your crown?" Netta says. Suddenly, she is seated in one of the dressing chairs and Mama is doing her hair. What the hell?

"You should've heeded your mother's warning, Jayd. She told you to listen to Netta and so did I. Now look at the price you have to pay for not honoring your crown." Mama spins Netta around in the chair and they're gone just as quickly as they appeared. All eyes are still on me, waiting for the next move.

Before I can plead my case any further, Laura walks over to Mrs. Sinclair, claiming the costume for herself. "Jayd, don't feel bad. It's better this way. Sometimes you have to be the martyr for the sake of everyone involved."

Mrs. Bennett hands Laura the dress and it's like she's being crowned right before my eyes and I feel stripped of my powers in the process. All I can think to do is cry and get the hell out of that room. Where are my friends?

Making my way outside, I find a quiet spot on the side of the drama room, facing Pacific Coast Highway. The fancy Mercedes Benzes, BMWs and other expensive cars are speeding down the street, passing me and my solitude by. But one car that doesn't belong slows down: it's Mickey's man. Out of all the people to run into when I should've been inside getting ready to make my grand entrance, it would have to be him.

Creeping up to the bus stop across from where I'm standing, he rolls down his window. He and Tre are in the car, just like they were yesterday when he harassed me. But this time I don't think he's looking for me. Feeling the vibe, I forget about my disappointment and pull my cell out of the robe pocket to call Mickey. Before I can dial her number to warn her and Nigel about the impending confrontation, Nigel's green Impala bumps loudly down PCH, turning in front of the same bus stop.

"That's that nigga fool," Tre says.

Mickey's man pulls his piece and fires three shots into Nigel's car.

I duck for cover and Nigel speeds off.

"Jayd, I thought you was trying to get up early so you can catch Mickey before school," Bryan says, interrupting my dream. Is it morning already? "And I need you to look at these bumps on my forehead. I think you pulled my braids a little too tight when you touched them up last night."

I was tense after my run-in with Mickey's man yesterday, but not as tense as Mickey's going to be when I confront her about it. No one makes me feel stripped like that, especially not so close to home.

"I'm up," I say, throwing the covers back and allowing the morning chill to wake me up. "And I'll get some of Mama's braid balm for your head." That's another lesson I learned from Netta's spirit book: never take your frustrations out on a client's head.

"Bet, little Jayd. The bathroom's all yours. You know where I'll be." Bryan leaves the door open and heads toward his broke-down van, parked near the side of the house, for his morning meditation. There are only a few steps between me and the back of the door where my clothes for the day are hanging, but from my comfortable spot in my tiny bed, it seems like a mile away.

My dream about Nigel and Mickey getting shot up by her man still has me rocked. I haven't had such a violent dream in a minute. I've definitely got to bring that one up with Netta this afternoon. And I hope the part about Laura taking my place as Lady Macbeth doesn't come true either. The whole dream was a mess and I'm not in a rush to retell it just yet.

Before I can make it out of my bed my cousin, Jay comes out of his room and rushes into the bathroom. Damn it, now I know this is going to be a rough day. Anytime I don't get in there before him it's a bad start.

"Jay, hurry up. I've got a bus to catch, unlike you," I say, making my way quietly into his room to retrieve my toiletries. Daddy turns in his sleep at the sound of Jay's loud peeing and my creeping. This house is way too small for comfort, if you ask me. But we're family, and that's just how it is sometimes.

"You can't rush nature, Jayd. Haven't you learned that in all of your studying with Mama?" he says, making light of what me and Mama do. As if she heard my thoughts, Mama clears her throat and shifts in bed, letting me know it's time for me to get moving.

"Don't worry about what I learn. You just worry about getting out of my way. Come on, move it," I retort, opening the bathroom door while he washes his hands. At least he's a clean dude, unlike our uncles. Even Bryan makes a slight mess from time to time. But since our schedules coincide I've been training Bryan and he's getting better at cleaning up behind himself.

"So impatient," Jay says, pushing past me and shutting the door behind him. He can be more of a drama queen than I can sometimes. Speaking of which, I better get into character if I'm going to deal with Mickey's ass today. I want to catch her first thing this morning and squash this madness. Her man is too unpredictable for me to let another minute go by without talking to her. I tried calling Mickey several times last night, but her phone was off, just as I predicted. No matter how big South Bay's campus is, Mickey can't run away from me at school.

My morning has been uneventful so far. My first two classes were a breeze—Spanish always is, and English is my favorite class. But if I don't get more work done on my paper, government class is going to be most uncomfortable. Our rough drafts are due today and I'm ready, but it's not my best work. I've been so distracted by my friends and their issues that I haven't focused on my own. Speak of the devil, here Rah goes texting me now.

Peace queen. I'm going to have my baby girl this weekend.
I want you to meet her. See you after school. Holla.

Rah finally wants me to meet his daughter. Wow, now I know he's maturing. If I could only get Mickey to grow up and take responsibility for her failed hustlin', then we might be able to save ourselves from her man's insanity before it goes any further.

I've been looking for Mickey and Nigel all morning, but they don't seem to be anywhere. I hope they didn't ditch again. It's too close to the holidays to get caught for something that stupid. Break is almost over and I should take the remaining time to get some work done in the library. I want to clean my locker out at lunch. It's gotten too overstuffed for me to handle.

When I get inside of the library, Mrs. Bennett's standing there talking to the librarian. I should've known her evil influence extends even this far. They both look at me crazy, and that's just fine with me. All I want to do is get work done before third period and get out of here. To hell with what they think or say about me. I've got bigger fish to fry today.

"Good morning, Jayd," Mrs. Bennett says, forcing me to speak. I'm not going to give her another opportunity to call me rude. "It was nice to see you at Jeremy's on Thanksgiving, even though you two aren't an item anymore."

Why is she so into my business? Doesn't she have anything better to do?

After taking my government notebook out, I slide my backpack across the counter to the librarian, who promptly puts it in the cubby and hands me a number.

"You left this last time you were in here," the librarian says, passing me the piece of paper. If I hadn't paid for it already, it would probably be in the trash, judging from her obvious disdain of the subject matter. It's the bibliography from Mr. Adewale's paper on voodoo queens. No wonder I didn't miss it. I'm more interested in the content than the references, but it's still good to have it all.

Mrs. Bennett can't help herself, glancing at the paper as I claim it. "Oh, researching more fiction, I see."

Mrs. Bennett is the snidest broad I've ever met. It should be illegal for teachers to be haters. But, like shoes, haters come in all colors and sizes.

"There's nothing fictitious about voodoo," I say, putting the fear of God in the librarian, but not in Mrs. Bennett. Her eyes glow as she smiles at me. Just like Esmeralda's eyes, Mrs. Bennett's give me the creeps.

Before she can get another remark in, I walk away from the counter, claiming my backpack number and heading out.

"See you in rehearsal," Mrs. Bennett says to my back.

I can't wait until this festival is over. I've always wanted a lead role, but not at this price. But, like Mama says, there's always a sacrifice when we're at the crossroads and dealing with Mrs. Bennett is mine.

Today is the first time in weeks I don't have rehearsal at lunch—well, at least not for the first half of it. The stage crew is performing a sound and lighting check for our first dress rehearsal. And Mrs. Sinclair won't be back until lunch is almost over, so I'll take this time to clean out my locker. Nigel and Mickey obviously don't want to be found and Jeremy and Chance have a Hacky Sack tournament in the parking lot, so I have no excuse for not cleaning out this hot mess. No wonder my life is so hectic; I'm anything but organized these days.

It's tough keeping it all together when I have to move around so much. Sometimes I wonder what it would be like to have a house with my own room. I could keep my letters and private notes in a box under my bed or in my closet, like normal teenage girls. My locker's packed with all kinds of paper: half pieces with notes scribbled on them, fliers from ASB and other school organizations advertising various events, loose papers from teachers. Luckily we have a recycling program on campus. Otherwise all of the paper use would be a real disgrace.

"What's up, Jayd? Spending lunch alone?" Misty says, walking out of the girls' bathroom with Shae behind her. I guess now that Misty's not a virgin she's cooler in Shae's eyes, even if her first sexual experience was a public nightmare.

"I thought you were afraid to look at me or something. Doesn't that include speaking to me?" I ask, looking at her briefly before rolling my eyes and giving my attention back to my locker. I glance briefly at the trash can next to the bathroom door and walk over to retrieve it. Having the trash can next to me will make the process fly by. Just then, Laura walks out of the ASB room, crossing my path on my way back to my open locker.

"You know what, Jayd? You're going to end up with no friends and everyone's going to know just how strange you and your grandmother really are. Watch and see," Misty says, sashaying her wide ass out of the main hall. Shae's probably too high to make any smart-ass comments of her own right now, and that's just fine with me. The less friction I have from them, the better. But Laura's not leaving without a few words of her own, I'm sure.

"You know, Jayd, I must admit, you are a very talented actress," Laura says, approaching my locker.

Ms. Toni and Reid are in the drama room serving as witnesses to the sound check. I wonder what Laura's doing up here all alone? That's very unlike her. And, her giving me a genuine compliment is even more suspicious.

"No wonder you were able to jostle your way into Lady Macbeth's crown."

"I didn't jostle my way into anything, Laura." I toss the trash into the bin, trying to ignore her energy. I have to deal with this broad enough as it is. I can't wait until next week when this festival is over. Sharing a class with Laura and the rest of ASB has proven to be more than a sistah can handle.

"Oh, yes you did," Laura says. "And the worst part about it

is that you did it with tricks up your sleeve. But believe me, little girl, you're not the only one who can work magic around here."

Again, Misty pops up her curly head out of nowhere, this time without Shae. Maybe she left something behind. Whatever the case, both of them and me in the main hall is still too close for comfort in my world.

"Damn, Jayd, how much shit you got in your locker? It's going to take you all day to clean that up."

Misty's got her nerve talking. The only reason her locker isn't as bad as mine is because she rarely takes notes or has extra paperwork to bring home. No one would ever accuse Misty of being a diligent student.

"What's in my locker is none of your business," I say, tossing the last of the miscellaneous papers into the can before slamming the locker door shut and returning it to its post by the bathroom door. I've got about five minutes before the bell rings and want to get to Mrs. Sinclair as soon as she lets us in. I'm too anxious to try on my costume to give these broads any more of my time.

"No, but once it's out and in the trash, it's public property. Remember that," Laura says, walking out of the nearly empty hall before I can make my exit.

What the hell was that all about? Misty, looking momentarily victorious for some reason, heads toward the main office, leaving me completely alone in the vast building. What the hell just happened here? Before I can figure it out, Chance texts me, telling me to get down to the drama room for my fitting. It's about time.

When I get to the dress rehearsal, everyone's already buzzing with excitement over his or her costume. The drama room is packed and there's more plastic garment covers on the floor than at a cleaner's as cast members and groupies alike uncover the precious wardrobe. I have to admit, anytime we perform a Shakespearean play, the costumes are amazing. I spot Chance, Matt, and Seth in a corner making fun of Chance's costume. He does kind of remind me of a character in *Men in Tights*.

"So, how's your injury, Banquo?" I ask, gently pushing Chance in the arm.

Alia's eyeing her witch costume in awe: it is pretty amazing, including a hump for her back, long, gray hair, warts and all.

"It's all good. Hey, have you seen Nigel today? I've been looking for him and texting him all day with no response."

Now I'm positive he and Mickey ditched. One day they're going to get busted for that shit.

"No, I've been looking for Mickey myself." I glance toward the door leading to the hallway where the dressing room, bathrooms, Mrs. Sinclair's office, and the entrance to the theater are. I want to go pee, but I notice Laura heading back that way and I've had enough of her for one day.

"Jayd, your dress is in the dressing room. The gown for the sleepwalking scene isn't ready yet, but will be by opening night," Mrs. Sinclair says, entering the classroom and buzzing through the packed room to check on all of the outfits. Her bushy, red head can be seen among all of the students with her checklist in hand. "I need everyone to come and sit down with their costumes in hand, please. Hurry so we can get class started and rehearse, please," Mrs. Sinclair shouts through the crowded room. As if she's said nothing, no one moves.

"Hey, get your clothes, sit down and shut up," Chance yells, making Mrs. Sinclair smile. If I didn't know better, I'd say he has a crush on our little teacher. I guess I'd better be obedient like everyone else.

When I get to the dressing room, Laura's eyeing her costume but touching mine.

"So, how long have you been a fan of Shakespeare?" Laura asks, delicately placing my dress across the dressing room chair.

"I'm not really," I say, watching her every move in the mirror reflection. What's she really up to? "Why do you ask?"

"Well, I was just wondering how a little ghetto girl like you would know how to perform a part from one of his plays. I figured you must've gone to camp like the majority of the drama students."

"No, I don't know of many Shakespearean theater camps that come through Compton. But I did see a crackhead throw her own baby in the Dumpster once. That provided, I think I've trained well for this part, don't you?" I actually heard about that happening, but Laura doesn't need to know all of that. The look on her face tells me my goal of shutting her up has been accomplished, at least for the time being.

I take my dress off of the chair, ready to take off the plastic, revealing Lady Macbeth's main attire. But before I can even get my backpack off, Mrs. Bennett enters the dressing room followed by Mrs. Sinclair, who's running around like a chicken with her head cut off. Laura gives me an evil eye and walks over to Mrs. Bennett, giving her a hug. Where is Ms. Toni when I need her?

"Mrs. Bennett, I don't know how this got into my purse, but it did and I wouldn't be doing my duty as a student-body officer and Homecoming court member if I didn't report it." Laura reaches in her Prada bag and slips out a small piece of notebook paper.

"How does being the ASB president's girlfriend make you an officer?" I ask. She takes herself way too seriously. No wonder she and Nellie get along so well.

"Whatever," Laura says, flipping her heavy, straight brown hair over her shoulder. "The letter's from Mickey to Jayd,"

Laura says, waving the torn paper in front of Mrs. Bennett and me. I see I'm not the only one who can hustle.

"How much of a coincidence is it that I just cleaned out my locker a few moments ago and now you've mysteriously popped up with a letter that was in my locker." I reach for the letter but Laura—being the Amazon girl that she is—does a good job of keeping it out of my reach before handing it to a curious Mrs. Bennett, who looks up from her reading long enough to give me a sinister smile. What else has she got up her sleeve?

"What's so serious about the letter that it needs my immediate attention?" Mrs. Bennett asks, opening the dilapidated note. Her thin, blonde eyebrows arch high, like she's just had a facelift.

I know I didn't have a letter from Mickey in my locker that would have any pertinent information in it, so I'm really not too worried. But who knows what evil has up its sleeve at any given moment?

"It's proof that birds of a feather flock together."

I look from Laura to Mrs. Bennett and realize I'm missing something. What the hell is Laura talking about? Mr. A and I already established that I'm a different bird, so I don't know what species she's referring to.

"Well I guess you fly with crows, you trashdigger."

Laura walks up to me, bends down and whispers in my ear. "I don't have to do my dirty work. I have others to do that for me."

What did that mean? And if she didn't have her backup, she'd already be picking her teeth up from the ground.

"Your friends Mickey and Nigel are under investigation for skipping class, and we think they had help in forging her mother's signature. We are taking the matter very seriously. And if your handwriting matches the signature on the letter, we will have to punish you as well." Mrs. Bennett looks elated at the content of the letter.

Goddammit, if Mickey ain't always getting me in some shit. What the hell?

"I don't care about all that. What I care about is you stealing my stuff. There are ways of going about getting what you want without jacking me," I say to Laura, who's looking down at me like she wants to slap me and I wish the bitch would. I'd give her ass a run for her money, even if she does stand a good eight inches taller than me and is built like a thin dude.

"Well technically, Jayd, trash is public property. And as you said, you threw this out." Mrs. Bennett's too much for me right now. "Is this your letter?"

"I don't know; let me see it." I put my hand out for her to give it to me.

But Mrs. Bennett folds her arms across her flat chest with the note in question clutched firmly in her hand. "We don't even have to go through all of this. If you simply admit to your role, we can avoid the embarrassment of taking it to the administrative level. Did you help Mickey forge her mother's signature and ditch, or not?" she demands. Mrs. Sinclair looks like she wants to help, but I know there's nothing she can do. Mrs. Bennett's way over her head both in terms of seniority and bitchiness.

"If you've got proof, you know the answer, then don't you?"

My smart-ass remark makes Mrs. Bennett's blue eyes turn red. Damn, I know I'm in for it now and I didn't even get to see my dress.

Ms. Toni, Chance, Matt, and Seth walk into the dressing room, ready to begin rehearsal, only to find more drama back here than they bargained for. Shell shocked, they all wait for the next move.

"Fine then, Jayd, have it your way. We can settle this in the principal's office. Come with me," Mrs. Bennett says, taking me by the arm and leading me out of the dressing room. The other students watch in shock as we make our way out of the drama room and up the hill toward the main office.

I can't believe this is happening. How did Mickey and Nigel get busted? The only people that knew about their ditch day were me and—of course—Nellie. This is a hater move that has hit me unfairly, and there's going to be hell to pay if I lose my part over this mess.

~ 6 ~
End Scene

"I working hard, I'm playing my part/
But the scene still won't work."

—DEBORAH COX

After spending the remainder of fifth period in the principal's office with Mrs. Bennett and missing the dress rehearsal, all I can think about is chewing Mickey's ass out. Mrs. Bennett wouldn't show me the letter, so I don't know exactly which one they have or if it's even mine. I have a funny feeling that the letter doesn't really say anything, even though Mrs. Bennett tried to make it seem like a confession.

I've seen plenty of cop shows where they interrogate the witness for hours to make them confess to a crime they didn't commit. Even if I did do it, which I didn't, I'm not confessing a damned thing, especially not to Mrs. Bennett. She can have all the proof in the world and I'll still deny my part in Mickey's mess. But Mickey can't get away with her hustlin' any longer. She needs to be called on it and now.

Since I missed fifth period, I really could care less about being late to sixth. While I was in the office, I saw Mickey and Nigel leaving the conference room. They looked like they had been in there all day. I know they were hungry, especially Mickey, so I'm sure they didn't go directly to class. If they did, I'll catch Mickey during the passing period and call her foul behavior out once and for all.

* * *

"Mickey, I need to holla at you real quick," I say, catching Mickey and Nigel in the main hall by her locker. She's snacking on some Oreos and chocolate milk; that used to be Rah's favorite drink. I can't wait to see him after school. But all pleasantries will have to wait until later.

"Jayd, I know what you're going to say," Mickey says, trying to defuse the situation before I get to her, but it's way too late for that. I'm already hot enough to set this entire school on fire just by thinking about this bull.

"You don't have a clue what I'm about to say or do," I say, stepping in her face, ready to get down with her. She and I have never had it out like this before. But I'm done with her taking advantage of me, and the people around us, for her benefit. Who does she think she is, Nellie?

"Jayd, they can't prove a thing. My mom and dad will never come up here for no simple shit like me ditching. They already know how I do. So, you're in the clear." She continues her munching as the bell rings in the empty hall, signaling the end of fifth period and the beginning of the student stampede. She nonchalantly steps away from Nigel, who's leaning up against her locker, ready to head to P.E., but we're not done.

"Yeah, and what about Nigel? Don't you think they might clear this with his parents, too?"

Nigel looks at me with distress in his eyes and I can see he's already considered that possibility. Nigel, like most sane kids, is still afraid of his mama and daddy—mostly his daddy. But at the moment, I think he's more afraid of losing Mickey, so he chooses to keep silent and walk it out.

"Jayd, Nigel's the star quarterback and he has a game tonight. They're not going to call his parents and say shit," Mickey says, a little too cocky for me. It's Nellie's job to keep Mickey straight, and she's been off the ball for a minute now.

"And what about my signature, Mickey? Mrs. Bennett says she can prove I signed the damned letter and that'll be all she needs to give my part to Laura." Just the thought of that witch in my costume makes my skin crawl.

"That bitch has always had it out for you, girl," Mickey says, stating the truth. But that's not the point. Mrs. Bennett wouldn't have shit to say now if it weren't for Mickey's mess. "That sounds like a personal problem to me."

"Mickey, I don't need any help getting into any more trouble with the administration. All I need is more drama and more ammunition for Mrs. Bennett to hate on me."

Mickey looks from Nigel to me and then back at Nigel, who kisses her on the nose for reassurance, even if he does look more concerned than she does. I guess they've already figured this one out.

"Look, Nigel's not going to say anything about us. We're good, Jayd. You worry too much."

This trick is really on one if she thinks I trust her or Nigel with my academic future against this lily-white administration up here. When it comes down to it, we're all in the same sinking ship, except for maybe Nigel, until after football season's over. And I know for a fact the folks in the office would love to see me go down, Misty and her mama included.

"Us? What us? There is no us. There's you and your selfish bull and me getting caught up in this mess."

For a moment, I think I've reasoned some sense into Mickey's hard-ass head, but her arrogant smile returns to her cocoa complexion, showing I haven't fazed her at all. She tosses her blonde-streaked weave over her bare shoulders— her Bebe off-the-shoulder top is fierce, I must admit—and sucks her teeth in disgust.

Oh, no she didn't. Now I'm really gonna call her business out and in front of Nigel no less, who's not going to like what I have to say at all.

"By the way, Mickey, your man paid me another visit yesterday and this time he wasn't so friendly."

Nigel's jaw tenses up and rightfully so. Originally, he's from the same hood as we are, so he knows her man's reputation. I don't know what Nigel was thinking, messing with a gangster's girlfriend anyway. Bryan hipped me a long time ago to the crazy fact that boys love danger and, according to my dream last night, Nigel's definitely got a volatile situation on his hands.

"You okay, Jayd?" Nigel looks genuinely concerned, but I can't tell if it's more for me or for his own ass, because I know intuitively that Nigel knows he's next. "Did you tell Rah?"

Before I can answer Nigel, my cell announces a text from Rah, saying he'll pick me up a little later than he'd originally planned. I'll have to call Netta after school and let her know I'm running late. I'll catch Rah up on all of the drama with Nigel, Mickey, and her man, as well as the rest of the day's madness on the way back to Compton this afternoon rather than text him back now. I want to squash this mess with Mickey right now.

"What are you talking about?" Mickey says, stepping back into Nigel's arms now that she thinks I've calmed down. But this is just the quiet before the storm. Speaking of which, students are rushing through the hall, knocking into me like I'm not even standing here. But I'm so vexed I don't even feel their pale bodies pushing mine. I see Maggie and the rest of El Barrio making their way through the busy hall, but she doesn't notice me. If my friends keep tripping like they are now, that'll be my next crew. From what I can tell, they always have each other's backs.

"What I'm talking about is you not caring about the people that are here to back you up each and every time you do something stupid. You need to check yourself before I have to, Mickey, for real."

Mickey laughs at my threat, pissing me off even more. I can feel my head getting hotter, and my eyes begin to shimmer like Mama's do when she's upset. I'm sure my brown eyes don't have the same luminous effect as Mama's green ones, but they're doing something, because both Nigel and Mickey are looking at me a little differently now. Nigel looks mesmerized by my eyes, and so does Mickey, but it doesn't keep her from speaking up.

"Jayd, you can do all the magic tricks you want, I don't give a damn. I'm not worried about the people up here and you shouldn't be either." Mickey looks at Nigel and regains his full attention. She grabs his right hand with her left and begins to head toward sixth period.

Why does she think I'm playing with her? "That's easy for you to say, Mickey. You've already got what you want out of life. Others, like myself, actually want to graduate with honors and go on to do bigger and better things outside of getting married and knocked-up." As soon as the words hit, I see Mickey's really feeling my heat. Well, it's about time. She should know better than to test me. I'm probably the only person in this entire school who's not afraid of her. That's why we're better friends than enemies because, once it's on and cracking between us, it's an even match for sure.

"Jayd, you sound just like your little hating friend Nellie right about now, and I'm not having this conversation again. You're tripping."

I follow them both down the long corridor leading to the exit and the gym. Ahead of us, Misty, KJ, and the rest of their weak crew are also leaving the main hall and heading for gym class. Lucky for me, my class is on the opposite side of the gymnasium from theirs.

"What's up, baby-mama and maybe baby-daddy?" KJ says to Mickey and Nigel as KJ and his crew lead the way down the hill. Nigel looks at KJ like he wants to slap the taste out of his mouth, but keeps his cool. He's better than me. My head gets hot just thinking about KJ's smart-ass mouth. "And aren't you supposed to be practicing your spells or something for your big opening night?" KJ asks, turning around to face me while walking backwards down the hill. If I focus hard enough on his shoes, maybe I can make him trip and fall. That would make my day.

"No. Apparently she's going to lose her part and it's all my fault," Mickey whines, making fun of my predicament, which is anything but funny to me. She gets a good laugh out of KJ, Misty, and their crew, at my expense, pissing me off even more, and Nigel doesn't look happy about her mocking me, either. What's gotten into her? I know it's more than the baby she's carrying. But if I could make bets on who the baby's daddy is by the way she's carrying on, I'd say the characteristics don't favor my boy Nigel at all.

"Damn it, Mickey. This is just the type of shit I'm talking about and I'm tired of your selfish bull," I say, not backing down from Mickey for a second, amusing KJ and crew even more. But I don't care who's watching our impromptu production. Mickey needs to take this situation seriously and I'm not going anywhere until she does. "Now I see how Nellie feels. All you think about is yourself, damn the consequences, even if those consequences end up burning your friends. Is that how it's going to be?"

Mickey rubs her belly, trying to gain sympathy for her situation.

Nellie, Laura, Reid and the rest of the ASB cronies file out of the gymnasium with Christmas, Hanukkah and Kwanza decorations in hand, ready to clutter the football field and gym alike with holiday crap. I love how this school tries to act like it's tolerant of various cultures, even if we all know it's a bunch of bull. A few days ago, Nellie was hating on Laura just as much as the rest of us, but now she looks like she's having fun. I guess she contracted the rich bitch virus again. So much for my crew being immune.

I know the holidays are supposed to bring out the cheer in people, but this holiday feels the opposite of festive to me. I can't believe Christmas is only two weeks away and I still don't have a car or friends to roll with. Nellie hasn't spoken to me since I checked her about Mickey's right to chill with Nigel, and now I'm regretting that conversation too. Ignoring us completely while she's with her Homecoming court, Nellie walks onto the field, glances our way and then turns her head and continues walking without so much as a hi. Wow, what a friendly gift. I hope Misty gets me the same thing.

"What consequences, Jayd? No one even knows what really happened."

Nigel looks at us. I know he doesn't want anyone to overhear us talking, especially not his coach. The bell's about to ring for sixth period and we all have to get dressed, except for Mickey. My dance instructor is cool, but we have recitals today and I need to warm up for my hip-hop piece that includes a mixture of West African dance. I need all the vigorous exercise I can get to calm my nerves after our unfriendly encounter.

"Nellie knows, and now that you've made an enemy of her she may be tempted to tell on us both just to wipe that smug smile off your face."

Mickey considers the possibility of our girl ratting us out and I see her expression soften slightly, but not enough for me.

"I could lose my part in *Macbeth* over this shit. Not to mention I don't want your man coming at me anymore. Fix your shit, Mickey. Fix your shit."

The bell rings, ending our conversation for now, but it's

far from over. We'll finish it this weekend because come Monday, I want this mess handled so I can concentrate on my part in the play, and not Mickey's madness for a change.

"Jayd, like I said before, you care too much about what these white people up here think about you. And as for my man, I'll talk to him. Okay?" Mickey says, ready to split up with Nigel and go to class.

I bet it's interesting to watch her and Nellie hate on each other in gym, although I'm sure Mickey is excused from regular activities now that she's expecting, and Nellie also seems to be excused from class to help ASB decorate. And they think I've got it easy.

"Problem, ladies?" KJ asks, with Misty hanging on tight right beside him. Del and C Money—or Money, as he's going by these days—are close behind them, as usual.

I guess last Sunday's loss didn't affect KJ's game after all. They haven't missed a beat of our conversation and I'm sure Misty's soaking it all in to report back to Laura. I suspect they are working together and I will prove it one way or another.

"I'll see you this weekend, Jayd. Holla at my boy for me." Ignoring KJ's last comment completely, Nigel kisses his girl before heading off to football practice. Mickey looks like she has something else to say to me, but holds her tongue for now.

"Mickey, I'll talk to you later," I say.

Mickey rolls her eyes and turns around to walk toward the east side of the gym where the girls' locker room is located. Misty wisely waits a few moments before following Mickey to change into her gym clothes. Walking toward the south side of the building where the dance studio is housed, Misty can't keep her mouth shut a minute longer.

"Looks like you're losing all of your friends, Jayd. What's going on?" Misty asks, mocking my troubled crew.

She's got nerve talking to me about losing friends. Misty

doesn't have any real ones that I know of, her present company included. When Mickey busted her out a couple of weeks ago for having the clap, no one had her back, not even KJ, who we all know gave it to her. Now she wants to talk shit to us?

"I see you've gotten a lot bolder since hanging out with KJ and Esmeralda," I reply, turning around to face my nemesis. I look her in the eye and notice that she's grown a good two inches since I last saw her. I look Misty up and down, noticing her high heels and short skirt. She's turning into her mother right before my eyes, and KJ seems to like the change.

"I don't need anyone to make me bold. I am what I am, just like you are what you are." Misty struts away from me as KJ tugs her hand tightly, indicating he's ready to go. I know he doesn't want to be too late for practice. KJ doesn't mind running extra laps, but even he has his limits for pushing the coach. Money and Del are already walking through the open door leading to the boys' locker room.

"Speak for yourself, Misty. I'm a *who*, not a *what*. Haven't you learned anything since you've been at this school, other than how to mess up people's lives with your big-ass mouth? Oh, I'm sorry. I meant with both your big ass and your big mouth." KJ laughs at my joke, but Misty's stoic look displays her low tolerance level for me.

"Your world is crumbling right before your eyes, isn't it, Jayd? First, you have no man. Then no part in the wack-ass school play. Now your girls are gone, too. What will you lose next, I wonder?" Misty's voice is cool and calm as she follows KJ away from me, which is very unlike her.

Besides KJ's poison, I wonder what else has gotten into her, for real. But even with her apparent case of split-personality syndrome, she doesn't scare me. Unfortunately for Misty, I know exactly who and what she is. And even on a bad day, Misty and her kin are no match for me and mine.

"It ain't over until the fat lady sings, and she hasn't even entered the building yet," I say, as she leaves. Wait until she sees what I've got in store for her. I bet she won't be talking so confidently after I'm done.

Let me get to class before Mrs. Carter notices I'm not dressing up. I'll leave the rest of the drama for next week. I'm going to sweat out all of this heat if I can and concentrate on enjoying a peaceful weekend. Maybe Netta can cleanse my head tonight, if she has time. I need clarity before I face Mickey again and meet Rah's daughter for the first time.

~ 7 ~
Baby-Mama Drama

"Now, how could you hustle me/
When I'm the one who really loves you?"

—CHANGING FACES

I had a good workout, but the heat from my confrontations with Mickey and Misty hasn't left my head at all. If anything, after my vigorous West African dance moves imitating a warrior, I really feel like chewing out Mickey, Laura, Misty, and anyone else who gets on my nerves today. By the time Rah gets here, I'm still going to be too pissed to completely chill, no matter how happy I'll be to see him.

The sun has come out in full force this afternoon, making my hike up the steep hill to the front of the main office even more draining after dance class. This is the best place to meet Rah, but it's also the most popular place to wait. I can't wait to start driving lessons next week and be in control of my own transportation. Until then, I am relieved Rah's agreed to be my steady ride to Compton during the week and Inglewood on Fridays. I'm glad our schedules match, since he likes to visit his grandparents on the weekends and he has to go back to LA afterwards, making it convenient to take me to Netta's and to my mom's.

I'm so glad it's the second to last week of school before the winter break. I need some time away from this place in the worst way. Starting my weekend out working with Netta is just what I need both spiritually and financially. I also have to do Shawntrese's hair and touch up Cedric's braids, so I'll have enough work to do to keep me busy until I get back to Mama's on Sunday. Kamal Rah's younger brother is spending the weekend at their grandmother's house, leaving Rah alone to get to know his daughter. I know Rah wants me to chill with him and his baby, so I will have that to keep me occupied, too.

"Waiting for Godot?" Laura asks, stepping out of the main office with Reid behind her, as usual. She thinks she's got it going on, and for a white girl at South Bay High, I guess she does.

"It's none of your damned business who I am waiting for," I snap, not looking up to meet her dull brown eyes. Unlike mine, her lifeless eyes don't sparkle like 50's bling.

"Poor, hostile Jayd. Always so testy. Nellie did warn me about your temper."

What the hell did she just say to me? And what the hell has Nellie been saying to her? "What does Nellie have to do with this?"

Reid and Laura walk past me down the steps and toward the curb where her black BMW convertible is parked.

Where the hell is Rah? The last thing I need is another confrontation today. I've had more than my share of heat for one day.

"Nellie's officially in our crew now," Laura says, like we're two parents fighting over custody of our only child. "So, all of her knowledge becomes ours." Reid takes the keys from Laura, pushing the alarm to unlock all of the doors and the trunk, where he places their backpacks and coats before letting the hard-top down. I don't blame them for wanting to get some sun because Lord knows they both need it, but it's not that warm.

"Look, one-of-zero, I don't know if you've heard of a little thing we humans like to call free will, but Nellie's good at exercising hers. If you need another member for your Borg crew, I think *Star Trek: The Next Generation* comes on at seven."

Laura, unmoved by my retort, looks at a laughing Reid, who's obviously amused by my joke. I knew Reid was a trekkie. He's probably a regular at the conventions and all.

"I didn't know you watched *Star Trek*, Jayd. That was a good one."

One cutting look from Laura silences Reid's momentary entertainment and I feel her. The last thing I need is Reid giving me props.

"Thank you, two-of-zero, but I don't need a cheerleader."

As if her ears were itching, Nellie steps out of the main hall with Chance by her side. I haven't talked to her since our disagreement about how she's dealing with Mickey and Nigel's growing family. If it weren't for Chance, I wouldn't know how she was doing at all, since she won't return a sistah's messages. What's really going on?

"Hey, Nellie," I say. Nellie looks at me, slurs a sorry "hello" under her breath and walks past me like she barely knows me. I know my khaki sweater-dress and hip-hugging blue-jeans isn't the flashiest outfit, but I know Nellie sees me sitting here. Laura smiles wickedly at me, pleased by her work. People can talk all the shit they want to about me. But from the looks of it, Laura's the real witch around here.

"What's up, Jayd?" Chance says, leaving Nellie behind and walking over to me. As he bends down to give me a tight hug, I can see Nellie roll her eyes at Laura, who gives her a signal like she's ready to go.

"Hey, boo," I say, returning Chance's hug. I have to admit, I've missed having affection from all of my friends, even Mickey's crass ass. The moment we were all united was a fleeting one. And I'd give almost anything to get my crew back on-point.

"I was worried when you didn't come back to class. Is everything okay?"

I've told Chance about publicly displaying affection for me, especially around Nellie, who's obviously lost her damned mind in more ways than I'd originally thought. But I'm grateful one of my friends has maintained his sanity amid the never-ending games played at this school. No matter what, Chance has always had my back and I love him for it.

"Yeah, I'm good," I say, looking dead at Laura. I want her to know her dirty tactics don't scare me one bit. All is fair in love and war, as they say, and I'm about to rock her world from both vantage points. I love my friends and my role as Lady Macbeth, and I'm willing and ready to fight for them both. So if it's a war she wants, then it's a war she's going to get. "You know I don't let these crows up here rattle my tail feathers."

"Well, you might want to adopt another philosophy, Jayd, because we're just beginning to pluck you," Laura intervenes.

Chance pulls away from our friendly embrace to give Laura a scolding look. Reid, Laura and Nellie slide into the shiny Beemer, ready to take off. Is Nellie leaving her man behind to roll with them?

"Laura, back off," Chance says to the back of Laura's big head. Nellie turns around to give Chance a look of her own, but its effect is not as powerful as Laura's is on Reid, which pisses Nellie off even more. "You've done enough damage as it is." Nellie's look gets even harder, signaling to Chance it's time to go.

What damage is Chance talking about? By the tension visible in Nellie's already-tight cheekbones, I have a feeling it's more than just a catchphrase. But before I can grill him, Nellie gets out of Laura's car, walks up to Chance, grabs him by the arm and leads him toward his Chevy Nova parked across the street, ignoring me the entire time. At the beginning of the year, Nellie wouldn't be caught dead in his classic ride. Now it's hers to claim and she's doing just that for all to see.

"I'll holla at y'all later," I call after them both. Even if Nellie's ready to feed me to the wolves, I know it's just a phase. She's always tripping over one thing or another. Lucky for her, I'm a good enough friend that I'm not going to give in to another one of her temporary insanity tantrums.

"Hey, Jeremy," Chance says over my head while opening the passenger door for Nellie.

I look behind me to see Jeremy walking out of the main hall. Is everyone on campus late today? Out of all the people walking down the steps this afternoon, I'm happiest to see Jeremy. Our schedules have been off, so he hasn't given me a morning ride to campus all week, and I do miss our stolen moments. Jeremy nods a "what's up" to Chance before directing his attention to me. He looks relaxed, as usual, in his faded navy Abercrombie & Fitch cargo pants, gray hooded Nike sweatshirt, and one of his signature baseball caps over his curly hair. I don't see how he stays warm in his worn Birkenstocks with no socks, but that's just how he rolls and it definitely works for him.

"By the way, Jeremy, Tania says to tell you hi and don't be a stranger," Laura slyly says, throwing her final verbal dagger at me before closing her door and fastening her seatbelt. I guess Jeremy's baby-mama drama will always haunt him as long as her friends are around to take up the baton in the hating marathon. Ignoring Laura's calculated comment, Jeremy waves bye to Chance and Nellie as they pull off behind Reid and Laura. I guess Nellie has a new hangout routine that doesn't include her old friends.

"Hey, Lady J. Do you need a ride home?" Jeremy asks, walking down the remainder of the steps and sitting down next to me on the last one. His blue eyes shimmer as he looks at me. If he were blonde, he'd look almost exactly like Samantha's last boyfriend on *Sex and the City*. Damn, why does Jeremy have to be so fine?

"Nah, I'm good," I say. I don't mention how I'm getting home because, by now, I'm sure he knows my Friday routine with Rah, and I don't want to rub salt in his invisible wound. "I didn't see you in third period today. Where were you?" I turn around, adjusting myself on the hard cement steps to face his tall frame. Thank God he decided to sit down. Otherwise, my neck would cramp up and that would be most uncomfortable later while I'm trying to do someone's hair.

"I just didn't feel like going today. That paper's getting on my nerves," he says, smiling his bright whites at me. "I made it to fourth, though." He sounds proud of his minor achievement.

Before I get too excited with him, Rah sends me a text with the exact opposite of what I want to hear right now.

Hey baby. Sorry to do this to you, but Sandy's tripping and causing a scene at my grandparent's house. I have to get over there now or my Granny's going to call the police. Can you catch the bus to work and I'll come get you after? I'm sorry baby. You know how it is. Luv u, Rah.

"Damn it," I say aloud. Ain't this some perfect shit? My first Friday working for Netta and not only am I late, but now I'm going to be hella late. I grab my backpack and take out the bus schedule in the small zip-up side pocket.

"Everything okay?" Jeremy asks, moving my weekend bag from in between us to his lap and scooting in closer to me. He smells fresh, like Irish Spring and expensive cologne. Jeremy's scent and overall presence seem to be calming me down. For the first time today, my head feels a little cooler.

"No, it's not. My ride just fell through and I was supposed to start my new job in five minutes," I say, looking at the time on my cheap cell, ready to toss it into the street. But, unlike Mickey, I don't have a man or two who will replace my electronic trinkets every time my mood changes. I'd better call Netta and tell her I'll be even more late than I'd originally thought I would.

"Well, I can give you a ride. Where to, Lady J?" Jeremy rises from his seat and places my black New York & Company weekend bag over his shoulder as if he knows he's going to be carrying it for me. He then reaches for my hand with his right palm open.

Why is he so sweet to me? And I still love it when he calls me lady. As I reach up, placing my hand in his much larger one, I fall back from the weight of the overstuffed backpack on my shoulders. All of the books in my bag are a testament to the massive amount of work I have ahead of me this weekend.

"I got you, Jayd." Jeremy puts his arms around my waist and grips me tightly, catching my fall. He looks down at me, focusing his blue eyes intently on mine. This feels too much like a kiss coming on and I'm not fighting the feeling. Rah's got to deal with his history and me with mine. But before we can get our smooch on, my phone vibrates, interrupting our flow.

Damn, who the hell is it now? I look down to see Netta's name pop up on my caller ID screen.

"Hello, Netta." I back out of Jeremy's embrace, much to his disappointment and mine. "I was just about to call you."

"Yeah, and say what? Where are you, girl? If you're not here in fifteen minutes, I won't have time to cleanse and train you before the Friday clients get here." Netta's regulars take up the entire weekend calendar and they are very particular. Tuesday, she showed me the schedule and everyone's individual hair box inside the cabinet. Netta doesn't believe in mixing up the clients' clips, combs, capes or anything else. And we have to be cleansed before we can touch anyone's head. Just like Mama, Netta's serious about her shit.

"I know, Netta, and I'm sorry. I've been waiting on Rah for the past forty-five minutes and he just sent me a message saying he can't make it to the school, but he'll pick me up after work. Now I have to take the bus to the shop and it won't leave for another ten minutes. But I'll be there as soon as I can."

Jeremy looks at me, grabs my hand and starts to pull me toward his Mustang parked across the street, near Chance's previous spot. I shake my head for him to stop, but he doesn't listen.

"Jayd, you'll never make it here in time, and my regulars don't like to be kept waiting. Just get here extra early tomorrow morning. You can help me get ready for a busy Saturday. Can you manage that?" Netta says, sounding half-pissed, but understanding, thank God. She knows a sistah has financial and transportation challenges. Even if Saturday's supposed to be my off day until I get a car, I'll make it to the shop tomorrow, come hell or high water. And Rah owes me for today, so I'm sure I'll only get a small protest from him when I ask him to be my ride.

"I'll be there with bells on. Thank you, Netta." Jeremy glares at me out of the corner of his eyes. He's trying to focus on finding his car keys in his many-pocketed pants while listening to my conversation. I know he's pissed that I didn't ask him to take me to Compton, but we've been over this already. I'm not ready to deal with being harassed by my hood folks for bringing home a white boy. And we're not even officially dating anymore, so why attract the drama?

"Uh huh," Netta lovingly grunts. "See you in the morning, little Jayd."

Convincing Jeremy to give me another chance is going to take more game than sweet-talking Netta. Mama and Netta have to forgive me for making bad judgment calls, but friends can be less forgiving and quick to turn on a sistah, like Nellie has proven this afternoon. What would I do without Mama and Netta consistently having my back, no matter how often I show out?

"Well, if you want to give me a ride to my mom's, I'll give you gas money," I say, hanging up my phone and following Jeremy to his baller ride. From the looks of the gleaming baby-blue paint and shining tires, I'd say he just got her detailed.

"Not a chance I'm taking your money. But I'll consider it payment enough if you let me take you out to eat, since you won't let me take you to work," he snidely remarks. "I feel like I owe you for keeping you from getting paid."

"There are so many things wrong with that statement, I don't even know where to begin."

Jeremy stops in the middle of the street to check his backpack for the keys. "Well, then don't start."

I like this slightly bossy side of Jeremy. I'm not going to protest too much because I am famished and all of the day's events have taken a toll on me. I knew he was holding back another part of his personality with me when we first started dating. Everyone's got to hold back a little: self-preservation is all a part of the hustle. He looks up at me and laughs at me leaning up against his ride. I'll let Jeremy go ahead and spoil me, for old times' sake.

"Okay, we can hang out, but only for a quick minute. You and I both have a ton of work to do." I pass him my backpack as he slips my weekend bag into the trunk.

"Tell me about it. My government paper topic has changed twice already, with the last one being the most difficult sale to Mrs. Peterson, but she finally approved it."

Jeremy walks around to the passenger's side and opens the door for me. I get in and reach across the soft leather seats to unlock his door, causing him to smile. He slides into his seat, closing the heavy door and pulling his seatbelt across his muscular chest. It felt good to be in his arms again and feels even better hanging out with him.

"Why is it so difficult?" I ask as he starts the engine. More than anything, I miss our conversations. I can talk to Jeremy about almost any topic and receive some interesting feedback. "There's plenty of information on Caesar. It's finding concrete information on my ruler, Califia, that's a challenge." The only information I can find outside of our family lineage is incomplete. I'm going to have to ask Mama for more suggestions when I get home on Sunday.

"Nah, I'm not doing it on him any more. I'm doing it on Barack Obama." Jeremy's choices never cease to amaze me. But I can't blame him for being interested in the Black politician. I'm interested in him, too. But my interests aren't all that professional.

"Why the sudden change of heart? Are you trying to get on Mrs. Peterson's bad side permanently?" I doubt she has a good side, especially since she's shaped like one of the Krispy Kreme donuts she loves to eat so much. But if she does have one, I'm sure Jeremy's on it. All the female teachers love them some Jeremy.

"Nah. I just got sick of reading about taxes and shit. That's all Caesar did: wage wars and raise taxes and that's not my idea of a good leader. Barack's got that cool-daddy, old-school hustler vibe about him that makes me want to know more about how he gets down. You feel me?"

If I didn't know better, I'd say Jeremy's been hanging around other Black folks besides Nigel and me.

"Yeah, that does sound kind of boring. Barack's definitely a more interesting topic than Caesar any day."

Jeremy laughs at my assessment of his paper topic. He turns the volume up slightly on his radio, releasing his right hand from the steering wheel. I envy his vehicular freedom.

"When I get my license, are you going to let me drive? I'm

taking lessons soon," I say, placing my left hand on the leather-covered wheel, ready to take over the reins if he lets me. Looking amused by my attempt to control the steering wheel, Jeremy lets go, momentarily surrendering his vehicle to me. I wish it had been as easy for him to do the same thing with his heart—that was our second problem. His baby-mama was, and remains, our first and most fatal issue.

"You see? You don't need a license for everything."

Before I can tease him about that loaded statement, my phone vibrates in my purse, giving us both a quick jolt. He regains control of the car as he flicks the right blinker. If we could give each other signals like that in life, we'd avoid a lot of accidents.

Why is Rah calling me when he just sent me a text a few minutes ago? Can he feel when I'm around Jeremy or what?

"Hey, Rah. What's up?" I say, trying to play it cool. "Is everything okay with Sandy and the baby?"

Jeremy touches my soft leather bag before turning into the busy intersection. I know he's happy I'm still sporting both the bag he bought me and the gold "J" bangle. It's been too cold to wear my bebe sandals and tank, but best believe I'll be rocking those, too, when the weather warms back up. The iridescent flakes in my puka-shell necklace send rainbow rays through the car—my latest gift from Jeremy. From the looks of it, I could still be seen as his girl.

"It's all good, for now. But you know how she is. I had to give her an hourly rundown of my schedule for the weekend. Sandy's unreal."

I feel his frustration. All we needed was for Sandy to come back into the picture. We had enough problems with Rah's ex-girlfriend Trish alone.

"No, Sandy's very real and that's part of the problem." Damn, did I just say that out loud? I'm really slipping. Rah and I are just getting to a place where we can be completely honest with each other. I don't want to ruin our progress with my sarcasm.

"Where the hell did that come from? I haven't had a chance to look at my calendar this month. You have to warn me, girl, when you're on your period."

Oh no Rah didn't go there with me. Even if it is time for my cycle to start, he has no right to assume that because I'm irritated it's my time of the month.

"Rah, I'm being rude to my ride. I'll holla at you when I get to my mom's house." I already sent text messages to Shawntrese and Cedric that their hair will have to get done tonight instead of tomorrow now that I'm going to be at Netta's shop all day. So Rah will have to wait until I'm done with my business to talk about his.

"Your mom's? What happened to working at Netta's?" Rah asks.

Jeremy's rugged jawbone flexes; he's obviously annoyed by my side conversation. I didn't want him knowing the intimate details of my relationship with Rah, but he's going to get the short of it right now.

"Your fictional baby-mama interfered with my plans," I say, saltier than I intended, but still making my point. With Rah, I always come after his other broads and their shit. Why can't I be first for a change? Jeremy looks at me again instead of the road, ready for some attention of his own and I'm ready to give it to him.

After a moment Rah breaks the silence. "Who's taking you to your mom's?"

Even though he's asking, I know Rah already knows the answer. I don't want to tell him Jeremy's taking me to Inglewood because he'll think I'm on a date, and then our weekend will be ruined. But I don't want to lie to him either. And why should I? If I have to get used to their baby-mamas, then Jeremy and Rah have to get used to each other, no matter

how jealous they get of me spending time with the other. And
Rah really has his nerve. He should know by now that he's
not the only one who has game.

"Jeremy."

After another quick bout of silence and my obvious impatience with the subject matter, Rah lowers his tone to try to
soften me up. But I'm embarrassed because I missed working with Netta for the first time without Mama, and for having this conversation in front of Jeremy. I'm way past the point
of being buttered up. The only thing Rah can do for me at
this point is let me go and pick me up on time in the morning. Anything else is extra I don't need.

"No matter what's out there, Jayd, you'll never find anything like what we've got. I know that and you know that.
Holla at me when you get settled in."

Rah hangs up the phone, leaving me to deal with his last
words while out with Jeremy. Damn, that brotha is good at
this love thing. I'm just learning the rules of juggling more
than one relationship, and it's anything but easy.

"Trouble in romance?" Jeremy asks, pulling up to a Chinese spot I've never been to before. I guess he's feeling different this evening. How did he know I have a weakness for
Szechuan?

"Just the usual drama." Jeremy knows firsthand what kind
of drama I'm talking about. Baby-mamas are no longer solely
a Black thing, and he's right in the mix with the other baby-
daddies. Chance is the only dude in my crew who doesn't
have a baby-mama, as far as I know. But anything's possible.

"Now do you see why it's better for Tania to go on with
her life? In the long run, I think it's better for the baby."

Damn, here we go again. I admit, Jeremy's life seems a lot
freer at first glance. But there's got to be a part of him that re-
grets his decision to let a stranger raise his baby. I know he
feels he didn't have much of a choice, since his father made it

clear that he'd disown any brown grandbabies. But still, Jeremy's not like his father and I feel like his conscience is eating away at him.

"Not really. You don't know how your baby's going to be raised or if he or she will be healthy. Don't you want to know anything?"

Parking in the crowded lot and turning off the purring engine, Jeremy puts his hands on the steering wheel, appearing ready to confess. "I put up a private trust for Tania and the baby so that they'll always have money, just in case her marriage doesn't go as planned. In return, she promised to send me updates on the baby. So, yes, I do care. But I still think this was the best arrangement, short of having an abortion."

Jeremy knows how I feel about abortion, so I won't even comment on that subject. It took a lot for him to tell me about their arrangement, and I'm glad he feels he can trust me enough to let me in.

"I knew you cared. I know you hate dealing with Tania, but I'm proud of you," I say, softening up.

Jeremy gently pulls me by the waist into his embrace, kissing me like he wanted to when were on the steps a little while ago.

Even while Jeremy's got me enraptured in his flavor, I can't help but think of how some girls just got it like that. I mean, their hustles are so tight any pimp would give them props. Tania's got a ballin' new hubby and a trust from her real baby-daddy. Mickey's got a man who won't even question the paternity of her baby and Sandy uses her daughter like a pawn on a chessboard to get what she wants from Rah. I'm not really hating as much as I'm just curious. My main question is how do some chicks do it? And, more importantly, how can I be down? I know Netta's got some golden advice on this topic and without Mama there to censor her tomorrow, anything goes.

~ 8 ~
Gold Digger

*"Now I ain't sayin' she a gold digger/
But she ain't messin' wit no broke niggaz."*

KANYE WEST

It's six in the morning and Rah is on his way. He must really love me to get up this early to take me clear across town on a Saturday morning. Jeremy wanted to come up after dinner, but I had too much work to do. When I got to my mom's house last night, Shawntrese and Cedric were chilling on the steps, awaiting my arrival. I sent Rah a text to let him know I was in, but didn't call him until I woke him up this morning. Rah hasn't looked at me the entire drive from my mom's to Compton. I know he's pissed about me hanging with Jeremy, but he'll have to get over it.

As we silently cruise down Greenleaf Boulevard toward the shop, the waning moon fading into the blue sky accompanied by the rising sun reminds me of relationships coming and going. Sandy and Rah, Tania and Jeremy, me and Rah and Jeremy. If it weren't for the drama with his baby-mama, Jeremy and I would probably still be together. Rah and I have always had our share of issues, so I'm not sure what it would take for us to be together fully. But Sandy being back in the picture doesn't help our relationship at all.

"How's your baby girl doing?" I ask, this time being the first to chisel away at the ice. He looks like he had a rough night and I'm not totally unsympathetic to what he's going through.

"Sandy wouldn't leave her with my grandmother last night without me being there. It was just a ploy to see me," he says, yawning as he cranks up the heat. The leather seats feel warm under my lavender Old Navy velour sweatsuit. With my gray Nikes to cushion my feet and complete my outfit, I'm all set to be comfortable for my long day.

It's less than two weeks before Christmas, so I know the sisters will be up in the shop in record numbers today, and that means good tips for me. I could use them, too. I intend on looking for a car after the first of the year. By then, I should have a few hundred saved to bargain for a halfway decent ride. My holiday motto is New Year, new ride and new ways of escaping drama, especially if it belongs to someone else.

"Yeah, Sandy's good at getting what she wants, no matter who it hurts," I say, remembering how she used to bait Rah, leading him to believe he was going to see his daughter, only for Sandy to show up without her. Back then he couldn't drive, so getting from one place to another was a struggle. Sandy would make Rah take the bus across town for nothing but an argument, mostly about money. I don't know why Sandy tripped. Rah always takes care of his seed, and the mama, too, which was always my problem with the whole situation. Sandy feels entitled to Rah's pockets because she has his child. But I think she needs to get her ass a job and stop living off of dudes.

"Sandy is good at creating drama, I know that. My grandparents are getting too old for this shit, but they were happy to see their great-granddaughter. I ended up leaving her over there to spend some time with them and my auntie last night. I don't care what Sandy thinks. She doesn't need to know all of my business." Knowing Sandy, she's one step ahead of his game, even if he's unaware of it. Her hustle is fierce when it comes to Rah and yanking his chain through their daughter. "I just got off the phone with an attorney my grandfather thinks might be able to help me get my baby."

"I'm glad your grandparents are being so helpful. Are they okay?" They've always had Rah's back, especially after his mother starting working the clubs—and her side tricks—on a regular basis. If it weren't for them, Rah and his brother wouldn't be able to stay in their house. Rah's grandparents are pretty well-off and own a few houses around our hood, which helps pay the rent on Rah's mom's pad. Rah makes up the difference and pays for everything else, including monthly child support plus some to Sandy through the state.

"Yeah, they're okay, but they've had it with Sandy's ass. They say she reminds them too much of my moms when she was young. I know she put my dad through a lot of shit with both me and Kamal." I can remember his parents arguing all of the time when Kamal was about Rah's daughter's age. Rah and I used to stay on the phone for hours every night back then and I could hear them going off on each other through Rah's end. That type of heat is never good and leaves a last-ing impression on the children involved.

"And you've had it with her too, haven't you, baby?" I touch his hand, softly caressing his ashy knuckles. I wish I could do something to ease his pain. But he made this bed and he has to decide how he wants to lie in it. I can only lis-ten and be a supportive friend. Anything else is out of my realm of desire.

I don't have the same instant-family daydreams Mickey has on the regular. I admit, when I first found out about Rah's baby, I wished I was the mother because I was in love with Rah in a different way when I was in middle school and as a freshman. By the time Sandy rocked her ghetto-fabulous way

into our world, Rah and I had been together for two years. I
didn't think anything could break us up, but that hussie did
it, and what makes it even worse is that I thought she was my
friend, so I really got to know her habits. I warned Rah about
her, but he never listens to me until it's too late.

"You don't even know, girl. I wish I would've listened to
you two years ago when you first met Sandy," Rah says, reading my mind. It scares me that we're so close. Rah closes his
eyes, taking my hand in his and inhaling my Bath & Body
Works lotion. He raises it to his lips and lightly kisses my fingers, then rubs my open palm across his smooth, chocolate
cheek. I like the way his short beard feels against my skin. I
can only imagine where we'd be if Sandy hadn't transferred
to Family Christian and entered our lives. But she did and
the rest is history.

"That's neither here nor there," I say, straightening up in
my seat. Rah has a way of making me forget why I'm not with
him anymore. He's got to stop feeling responsible for each of
his former girlfriend's well-being. Otherwise, he might as well
just call it a harem and get it over with. At least that way I'd
know exactly where I stand with him.

"What do you mean? You make it sound irrelevant that
you warned me about her ass from jump." Rah tugs uncom-
fortably at his braids under his black do-rag. I have to make
time to hook up my boy's crown. From the look of his wrinkled sweats and T-shirt, I'd say he rolled off the couch and
came straight to my mom's to pick me up. I know Rah feels
slightly responsible for me too, but I need to be first if he's
serious about making us work. The other two broads don't
deserve his time or money.

"I'm just saying it's in the past. You don't have to feel
guilty about that anymore. As a matter of fact, you should
stop feeling guilty, period. You don't owe me or Sandy anything—just your daughter, and you take care of her. You're

not Captain Save-a-ho, so let's move on." I stare at Rah, who's searching my eyes for something more. I know he feels the pain evident in my voice, no matter how sarcastic my words are. But my mom always says that guilt is a useless emotion that does more harm than good. And we have enough negative shit to deal with without Rah bringing more on his head than necessary.

"And I'm just saying that as a friend, I shouldn't have dismissed you like I did back in the day. And, as my woman, I was stupid for risking our relationship in the first place."

Rah stops at the red light and looks around for other cars. There are none. We're only two lights away from Netta's salon. Smiling at me, Rah pushes my ponytail from the left side of my neck to the right, bending into my neck and kissing me, soft at first and then harder, which he knows is my weakness. If he keeps this up, I'm going to have a hickey and I don't need that on my conscience again.

"Easy there, partner. The light's going to change and so is my skin if you don't quit." Rah laughs at me trying to push his one hundred and eighty-five pound frame off of me. I look at his tired eyes, seeing the sadness behind his temporary smile. I wish I could make everything better for all of my friends. I'm going to have to find something to help us all out of this funk we're in.

"You're right. I need to stop playing." And just like that, Rah's thoughts, like mine, return to the current problem at hand.

"Did the attorney sound hopeful about the situation?" I ask, trying to lighten his load. If I'm thinking about his parents, then Rah must be thinking about them, too. I wish he could go to Atlanta to visit his dad in prison for the holidays, but we don't have that kind of cash or time at the moment. So much for wishful thinking.

Rah's never gotten over his parents' relationship or his father getting locked up on his third strike, especially when the first two were because of disputes between Rah's mother and father. I have a feeling that's why his mother doesn't come home when Rah's there. Ever since his dad got locked up, she and Rah have had a tumultuous relationship at best. It also doesn't help that his mom chooses her men by how much money they've got in their bank accounts—another quality she and Sandy share.

"Yeah, the lawyer sounded hopeful as long as he gets his retainer. He says the first step is to take a paternity test, but you know Sandy's not having that. That's why when we go shopping tomorrow I'm going to take us to one of those places real quick and get that ball rolling. I'm not missing another precious moment with my girl."

"As you shouldn't. Time's the one thing we can't get back," I say as he pulls into the empty parking lot in front of Netta's Never Nappy Beauty Shop. Rather than leaving the neon shop sign light in the window like she usually does, Netta left the Christmas tree on all night, which has enough lights on it to light up the entire block. Netta loves the holiday season just as much as Mama does. I can see her salt-and-pepper hair bobbing through the window as she prepares the shop for a hard day's work. I'm looking forward to being her apprentice.

"I wish I could go back in time. You know I would've waited for you to be my only baby-mama if I could do it all over again." Rah cracks a smile before turning off the engine, ready to escort me inside.

"As romantic as that sounds, I'm glad I already dodged that bullet."

"You can't dodge it forever." Rah pulls me into a deep kiss before we get out of the car. I can feel Netta's eyes on me, but Rah's lips have always pulled me in.

"We'd better go. I've been late since yesterday afternoon, remember?" After a few more pecks, Rah separates his lips from mine and we both catch Netta's spying eye in the window. We step out of the car and into the brisk morning air. Even in Compton—where there's no snow—I can feel Christmas in the air.

"Good morning, Ms. Netta," Rah says through the closed iron front gate.

Netta buzzes us in. She looks up and rolls her eyes at us both. The smile peaking through at the corners of her mouth lets me know she's cool, just ready to get the day started and I'm with her. I've given Rah enough of my time.

"How are your grandparents, Rah? I haven't heard from your grandmother in a month of Sundays." Netta used to do her hair on the regular until Rah's grandmother stopped driving after her sight went bad. Now one of the neighbors does her hair and, in my opinion, she should have the neighbor give her a ride over instead of letting her touch her crown.

"She's doing well, ma'am. She misses coming to your shop, though." Rah looks around at the festive decor and can't help smiling at the cheery surroundings. Netta always has that effect on people. I believe she can make the devil itself smile out of pure joy.

"Well here, give her some of this braid balm. I'm sure she's run out by now." Netta walks over to the large cabinet that takes up an entire wall of the shop and opens one of the seven full-length doors. She looks up to the top shelf and pulls out a box with Mrs. Carter's name on it. She keeps all of her clients' tools, just in case they come back. "Tell her if she needs anything at all, I can send it through you or Jayd until she can get back over here."

"Thank you, and I'll let her know." Netta looks at Rah and I as if to say "okay, say your good-byes and let's get moving." Equally catching the vibe, Rah makes his way back to the front door. "Have a good day and bring me my money."

"You ain't my daddy, fool," I say, opening the door to let him out. He leans into me and kisses my nose.

"Not yet, but I'm working on it."

Rah thinks he's so slick. I push him out of the door while he takes his vibrating phone out of his pants pocket. Who the hell's calling him this early? He answers my question without me having to ask.

"Nigel's leaving my house now and wants us to meet up at the Westside Pavillion to go Christmas shopping after you get off. I'll be over my granny's house sleeping, so just text me when you're ready to roll."

The last thing I want to do today is fight my way through the holiday crowds at the mall. "I'm going to be working all day. Can we go shopping tomorrow? Everyone will be at church and we'll be able to get more done." I would really rather stay out of the malls altogether, being it's the second to the last weekend to shop for Christmas crap. And, no one's getting any presents from my broke behind, so why should I go and look when I have no money to spare?

"You're the boss, Queen. I'll let him know we'll catch up with him and Mickey tomorrow. I'll just take my baby to get our test and pick you up later."

"Mickey? Are you sure that's a good idea?" I assume he's aware of the argument she and I had yesterday. I'm sure Nigel filled him in.

"Yeah, it'll be cool. He says Mickey's not tripping off of that anymore, but I am. How come you didn't tell me her man's been trying to push up on you? I'm going to have to have a word or two with that nigga."

"And that's exactly why I didn't say anything." I step through the front door so Netta won't hear us. "The last thing you need is a confrontation with that fool. You've got your baby to think about, Rah. Besides, Bryan was there to handle it for me and I'm not afraid of him." I look inside to see Netta head to the back of the shop.

"Well, you should be. He's nothing to play with. I tried to tell Nigel that shit, but he didn't listen either. But now he's coming after you and you know I can't have no more competition. You already letting this white boy hang around too much as far as I'm concerned."

I knew he wanted to say something about me kicking it with Jeremy, but he's held his tongue so far. I don't have time to get into it with him right now about any of this stuff. "I'm looking forward to kicking it with you and your daughter, Rah. Let's stay in that moment, shall we?" I reach up and give Rah a big hug before heading back inside. Maybe I'll have more clarity about how to deal with everything after working with Netta all day.

When I step back inside, the shop's lights are off and the candles are burning throughout the cozy space. Incense and sage are burning in the four corners, cleansing the air. The African drums and soft, Cuban male voice drifting through the speakers in the ceiling take my mind briefly off of my own drama, centering me on my new task.

"I'm glad you could make it this morning, Jayd. We have work to do and it starts at the shrine. Put your things up and change."

I've been waiting to get back to the picture hanging above Netta's shrine. The woman at the river has been haunting my thoughts on the regular.

"Yes, ma'am," I say, putting my purse down in the cabinet with my name on it. I retrieve my personalized pink apron from the hook along with a clean white scarf to tie around my head. I drape the opening for the apron over my head, careful not to mess up my ponytail. I then tie the scarf over my smooth waves, ready to get to work.

"And when we're on the clock, you can call me Ms. Netta. It gives us an air of professionalism, okay?"

Nothing about this shop screams professionalism, but I'll play along. Now is probably the best time to ask Netta about my problems with Rah, Sandy, Mickey and Nellie. I'll take advantage of the quiet time before the shop's crowded with clients.

"Ms. Netta," I say, sounding sweet as honey, much to Netta's liking, judging by the big smile on her face. She leads us into the shrine room, passing me a brass bell and a mason jar full of water as I cross the threshold. "I need to talk about Rah."

Netta silences me by putting her index finger up to her lips and closing her eyes. "Not now, baby."

She walks toward the east corner of the room and lights the first of five white tealights on the different levels of her tiered shrine. The candlelight brings a warm glow to the tiny room behind the main shop and helps to set the tone for our entire day. Most would see this as a storage room or an office space. But in Netta's shop, this is where the magic begins.

"Get on your knees, Jayd, and give your head to Oshune," she says, pulling me down beside her.

"Can I ring the bell?" I ask, feeling like I need a little help giving my worries away. I've got too much on my mind to let it all go just like that.

"Yes, little queen, ring away. Whatever helps you let go of that load you carried in with you this morning is alright with me." Netta takes the mason jar away from me, freeing my hands up to ring my bell. She opens the lid, dipping her fingers in the water and splashing my face several times. "You can't touch anyone's head until you clear yours."

"But that's why I wanted to talk to you. I have a lot going on and I need help sorting it all out," I whisper as I gently ring the sweet-sounding bell. I feel like if I talk too loud I'll offend the spirits of everyone living up in here. And from the chills on my arms, there are more present than I can proba-bly count on all of my fingers and toes. At first glance, it ap-pears that the lady in the picture is swaying to the sound of the music, before refocusing her gaze back to her reflection in the water. Working here is going to be a trip.

"Sometimes the best conversations are had in silence. Some of the best wisdom is attained by simply listening. You'll see."

The doorbell rings announcing the first arrival.

"Okay. So, how do I get the day started?" I ask, following her lead as she rises from her station on the floor.

"You can start by cleaning the shrine. Then follow the in-structions marked in the spirit book for each client's prod-ucts. They are very specific, so pay close attention. When you're done, you can come out and help me in the front." It's going to take me all day to finish these orders. "And don't worry. You'll get all the advice you need from the ladies in the shop. Get busy, girl. We've got a long day ahead of us."

Netta's morning candles have melted down all around the shop, creating a soothing ambiance throughout. Netta serves brunch during the weekends as well as snacks, tea, and coffee throughout the day, all compliments from her and Mama's kitchens. She doesn't allow any other food or drink to be consumed in the shop and makes it known through the vari-ous signs posted on the walls.

Cleaning up and filling the clients' orders took up the en-tire morning, but it felt good to busy myself with Netta's spirit book. I also got to listen to the candid conversations between Netta and the several clients that have come and gone in the four hours we've been open. It's only eleven-thirty and I'm already tired, with about seven more hours to go. I don't know how Netta does it, but she works the entire weekend like this and never complains about it.

The most interesting conversation came up when a young single mother who's a relatively new client of Netta's came in to get her press touched up. She has a long weekend planned with a few different dates and made the mistake of letting the women know. Once she left, the real conversation began. They called her everything from a prostitute to a gold digger and then some. I asked how they were defining gold digger and we've been on the topic ever since.

"Words are tricky, little girl. Gold digger originally came from Mama Oshune, ain't that right, Mrs. Jenkins?" Netta points the skinny comb at me before parting her client's scalp.

"Mmmhmm," Mrs. Jenkins hums, nodding off to heaven, I assume. She looks so peaceful in Netta's chair. I hope I have the same effect on my clients. She's got this elder, Christian sister giving praise to a Yoruba deity right before Christmas. That's how powerful Netta's comb is. Netta leaves her station to check on Mrs. Robinson and directs me to take over Mrs. Jenkins's head temporarily.

"A gold digger was a beautiful, powerful, independent woman who only dealt with men who were equal to her. Your great-grandmother Maman Marie was said to be one, and your grandmother, too."

It's a bit strange being here without Mama to censor Netta. Who knows what she might say next.

"Yes, that's what I remember," Mrs. Robinson says from under the dryer. How can she keep up with a conversation surrounded by all of that noise and heat? That's why we keep the magazines there, so folks can read instead of trying to talk. "Your grandmother was something else back in New Orleans."

About eighty percent of the original Black population in

Compton is from the south. And the majority of Netta's clientele and Daddy's church members are from either Texas or Louisiana.

"Me too. My grandmother used to tell stories about that Maman Marie," Mrs. Jenkins says.

She better not say anything cross about Maman or I'll heat this oil up and burn her scalp.

"She was supposed to be the prettiest, green-eyed gold digger around town. Them Creoles always could snag a man with little effort, no matter who he rightfully belonged to." Mrs. Jenkins flinches at the extra-hot oil dripping onto her scalp, but continues with her hating. "Ooh, them Creoles work my nerves, with their privileged, high-falutin' airs and such."

Mrs. Jenkins sounds a lot like jealous to me, but I wouldn't dare say that aloud to an elder. Because these women and others in their hater's club have boring lives, they spread rumors about fascinating women who live their lives, no matter what anyone else thinks or says. That's why they all know about my grandmother, the last real voodoo queen in New Orleans. Mama's always made tongues wag, but they're still talking about when she left the Big Easy with my grandfather. His original church members say she cast a spell on him to get her hands on his money. But that, like most talk out of haters' mouths, was a vicious lie that Mama's had to live with ever since.

"Not all pretty women are gold diggers and not all Creoles are conceited. Now, can we please talk about something more productive, like what y'all are buying me for Christmas?" Netta comes to my rescue again, knowing I've had enough of this conversation.

I have personally noticed that folks from New Orleans consider themselves separate from the rest of the south, Mama not included. She moved around a lot in her childhood after her mama died and her daddy mysteriously disappeared. She spent some time in Arkansas and Texas with her grandfather's kin, as well as the surrounding states. It wasn't until she was about ten or eleven that Mama moved in with her father's sisters and learned about the voodoo lineage running through both sides of her family. Even if she is Creole by blood, Mama's southern by hood, and she's proud of all her roots.

"Mama has lots of haters and I feel her," I say, unable to hold my tongue any longer. The three ladies stop gossiping and look at me, doing the math in their heads. So they don't hurt themselves, Netta fills in the blanks, giving them their answer.

"Now, you know you can't say nothing bad about Lynn Mae in this shop and get away with it, especially not in front of her grandchild," Netta says, coming to Mama's defense like a good homegirl. My girls could learn a thing or two from Mama and Netta's friendship. With Mama's reputation around here, a lesser friend might not have wanted to stay associated with Mama for fear of losing business. But Netta's down for Mama no matter what.

"Is that right?" Mrs. Walker, the shortest of three clients in the shop this afternoon, says from her seat at one of the two open dryers. The three ladies are still looking at me as if they've seen a ghost.

"So this is the infamous Jayd," Mrs. Robinson says, looking up from her book to give me a once-over before allowing me to lift her now-off dryer and work on her scalp.

Netta warned me people would do this once they found out who I was. She told me not to worry about it, as most people think they know me and my grandmother by all the bull they've heard and that I shouldn't sweat it. Mama says like with most bitches, their barks are much worse than their bites. I wish Sandy were that type of bitch.

"Well, why didn't you say something when we were talking about gold diggers? It's in your blood, child," Mrs. Walker says, making the other two members of her trio giggle at my and my ancestors' expense.

How does Netta keep a cool head around these cackling hussies? Women like these are the reason Mama left the church years ago and never looked back.

"It certainly is," Netta says, taking over the conversation. I meticulously part Mrs. Robinson's flaky scalp, applying her weekly hot-oil treatment, specially prescribed and made for her. All of Netta's clients have their own combination of products to maximize their full glow. "As a matter of fact, it can be traced back to her great-ancestor, Queen Califia, ain't that right, Jayd?" Netta gives me a sly look through her reflection in the mirror, letting me know this isn't an innocent line of questioning, but more like one of my pop quizzes. "Why don't you tell us about her and her relation to the gold found in this state."

As I put Mrs. Robinson back under the dryer, I say, "Well, Califia—the famed Black queen of California—actually brought the gold with her from West Africa. She and her folks buried it all over the land and dug it up when she needed it, thus earning the nickname gold digger. When Cortez got here, he raped her and the land for the gold, enslaving her in marriage and taking her gold." Unfortunately, Cortez was an original pimp.

"That's not how I heard it," Mrs. Walker says, turning around in her seat to look at the decorations hanging from the ceiling. The crystal angels light up the already radiant shop, sending orange and red rays bouncing from the mirrors and off the walls. The Cuban music has faded into jazz, easing us into the evening. "I heard she tried to cajole Cortez out of the gold he found when he got there. She had the good stuff and gave it up easy and he not only gave up the gold, but named the whole damned state after her. Now we have to live with it."

"You heard wrong, didn't she, Jayd? People are always misconstruing the origin of names. Take the name of my shop for example," Netta says, ready to check everyone with a history lesson of her own. Ready for one of Netta's stories, the ladies settle down and give her the floor. Mrs. Robinson lifts her hair dryer after the bell rings, indicating it's done. She walks over to the Christmas tree and bends down, looking for a gift with her name on it, I assume.

"I like the name of your shop," Mrs. Walker says, trying to get back on Netta's good side. "I never want to be nappy again. My man likes a smooth head and I like my bills paid, you know what I mean?"

Sounds to me like Mrs. Walker has a hustle of her own going on. She's got her nerve calling my folks gold diggers. But I don't have to say a word. I'll just concentrate on Mrs. Robinson's scalp and let Netta check the elders.

"Nappy. Where the hell did that word come from, Jayd? I'll tell you where it came from—slave masters, that's who. I was a pickaninny and all that, growing up. And when I saw myself in the mirror, I didn't like my reflection at all. Then, because of Oshune's grace, I began to love myself beyond the name calling." Netta spins Mrs. Jenkins around in her chair to eye her work, which is perfect, as usual.

"All I'm saying is that women have to work to keep a man and to get the good ones in the first place. But there are some women who've got certain skills that decent women put limits on."

Mrs. Walker's right. Some sistahs will do anything to get a man, especially if they think he's got money to spend on them. I have to separate myself from the rest of the crowd. My gold belongs to me and can't be usurped by anyone. Besides, there's a thin line between being a ho and being a pimp, and I intend to stay away from both ends of the spectrum. I'll enjoy Rah without the expectations that come with being taken care of by him, and Jeremy too. The only gold I'm digging for is my own. I just have to figure out a way to avoid being hurt by the women around me who don't share my sentiments, Rah's baby-mama being the first on my list to deal with today. I'll deal with Mickey tomorrow.

~ 9 ~
A Hustlin' Hussie

"Simple love's hard to come by/
I'm just living my life, and I'm trying to be a lady."
—CHRISETTE MICHELE

After dealing with a few more clients, Netta and I cleaned the shop, closed down the shrine and now we're ready to go home. Rather than wait with Netta and her husband while they puff on their cigarettes, I choose to chill up front. Rah and his baby girl should be here any minute. Usually babies love me, but this time is different. I'm nervous about meeting Rah's daughter.

When Rah pulls up, I notice the beautiful baby girl playing in the backseat. He's bought a brand new Eddie Bauer car seat for her to ride in. It's only the best for his little girl. Finally, I get to meet me Rah's baby girl.

"Rah's here. Bye, Netta," I say, waving at her and her husband parked on the side of the shop not far from me. "And thank you for letting me come today. I learned a lot." I also made my own hair sheen spritz. When I saw how glossy Mrs. Jenkins's hair looked after Netta sprayed it on her do, I had to hook myself up with a personal sample.

"No problem, little queen. And you did good. See you Tuesday," Netta says as their silver Ford pickup pulls off down Greenleaf toward the farms.

"Hey Rah. Who is this stunning princess?" I open the door, placing my purse on the floor before getting in and turning around in my seat to face this little girl I've been hearing so much about. I quickly close my door to keep the cold evening air from entering the warm vehicle.

"Rahima, this is my girl, Jayd. Jayd, this is my baby girl, Rahima."

Rahima looks at me curiously, taking in all of my facial features. I smile at her, doing the same thing myself. She mirrors my delight and I know I've won her over. And vice versa.

"I don't know about being your daddy's girl, but it's nice to finally meet you," I say, reaching into the backseat to shake her chubby hand. Her tiny fingers grasp mine tightly as she smiles and tries to taste them. Rahima's finally real to me. "I've heard so much about you."

"If she could, she'd say the same thing about you. Isn't that right, baby girl?" Rahima gives her daddy a big smile. They look just alike, beautiful smiles, dimples in their chocolate cheeks and all. The only thing she got from her mama is the lightening of her cocoa complexion. Even Rahima's eyes belong to Rah.

"I hope it's all good stuff your daddy shared with you." I turn around and sit properly in my seat. Pulling my seatbelt across my lap, I look up at Rah, who's staring at me intently. Without saying a word, Rah pulls off toward the freeway, heading back to his house. I had a great day at work and am looking forward to a cool evening with Rah and Rahima.

"I rented some movies. I'd thought we could kick it at my house, order a pizza and just chill. Sound good?"

I lean back in my seat, reach behind to tickle Rahima's thick legs, and nod in approval of tonight's game plan. I couldn't have planned a more perfect night myself. To think Rah and I stopped talking when I found out he was hiding Rahima from me. Now, here we all are. Life's a trip and then some.

* * *

After spending all evening with Rahima and Rah, I am in love with the little girl. Rah couldn't deny her if he wanted to. She's the spitting image of her daddy, only a few shades lighter. Now I see why he never needed a paternity test to prove his fatherhood until Rah decided to go after full custody. Now here we are Christmas shopping with our best friends like the couple we used to be. We decided it would be a good way for me to make peace with Mickey, although I was reluctant at first. I'd rather just spend the day with Rahima and Rah, but making up with Mickey's important too.

From Rahima's calm and cheerful demeanor, I'd pay to get a maternity test if there were such a thing. Sandy's crazy ass doesn't fit anywhere in their picture-perfect family. At least Sandy let Rah pick out the name. Rahima's and Rah's names even mean the same thing: compassionate and merciful. It was also a way of permanently linking him to the baby, which was for Sandy's benefit more than a sweet thing to do. Sandy never does anything without thinking of herself first, kind of like how Mickey rolls.

Mickey and I haven't made up completely, but her checking her man for harassing me is a step in the right direction. But she still has a lot more ground to cover before we're completely cool again, starting with my signature on her letter. Mickey and Nigel need to take the heat off of me and the rest of their friends for their mistakes.

"Jayd, you're not going to lose your part in the stupid play," Mickey says, looking at the Hot Dog on a Stick menu. Rah, Nigel and Rahima are seated at a nearby table. "To let Chance, Matt, and Seth tell it, you're the best thing since sliced bread." Mickey orders for all of us, knowing what we each want. But there's a new addition she failed to include.

"And a cheese on a stick, fries and a small strawberry

lemonade please." I pull out the twenty Rah gave me to pay with and hand it over to Mickey.

"Damn, Jayd. Are you sure I'm the only one eating for two around here?" Mickey says, rubbing my belly. I am slightly bloated because I'm on my cycle, but my little pot belly is nothing compared to Mickey's bulge. If she wanted to, she would make a cute but pregnant Mrs. Claus, unlike the other imitators around the mall today.

Santa's helpers, elves, reindeer and the man himself are out in full force this afternoon. The mall's crowded and loud, with Christmas carolers singing loudly in every department store. My favorite holiday theme is in Macy's. They have a very modern Santa's Village look, with gold and white as their main colors. The ten-foot tree is covered with gold ornaments and the most stunning black angel was at the very top instead of the traditional star. The angel was so pretty I had to buy it for Mama.

"No, fool. You forgot to order for Rahima," I say, looking over my shoulder to see Rah walking his daughter around the table with his hands without getting up himself. He's such a good daddy. Too bad he's had bad taste in girls in the past.

"But you didn't, did you, Mama Jayd?" Mickey takes the receipt and change, handing it all over to me. The guys always take turns paying when we go to the mall and because Rah's with me, I'm in charge of the money.

"Don't call me that. I'm not her mother."

"No, but you know that's what she's going to be calling you soon enough. Mama Jayd, pick me up! Mama Jayd, can I have some candy?" Mickey says, mimicking a bratty child, probably much like the one she's going to give birth to.

"Whatever, Mickey. All I know is that if I lose my part, you have to name your baby after me, I don't care if it's a boy either," I say, pushing Mickey in the arm. The Westside Pavilion is definitely a mall for the well-to-do. I rarely get to come this far west into the city and am glad for the chance. Mickey, on the other hand, has complained the entire day because this mall doesn't have the same stores that are in the Fox Hills Mall. But the food court has her favorite mall foods, so she's content for now.

I'm too caught up in Christmas shopping for Rahima to care about much else. I went a little crazy walking through Macy's when Rah and Nigel took her with them to look at the latest video games. I was supposed to be going to the bathroom and ended up purchasing some cute dresses for Rahima that were on sale. I didn't know her size exactly, so I got them in a three-toddler. That way she can grow into them if they're way too big.

Nigel walks over to help me carry the trays of food back to our table. With him around, Mickey doesn't have to lift a hand. It must be nice to have a man who worships you like Nigel does Mickey. I know his ex-girl Tasha's hating on Mickey big time. She lost out, for real. If I know girls, Rah's ex Trish is providing her girl with all of the details of Nigel and Mickey's love affair like a true best friend.

When we all sit down, ready to grub, Rahima's the first one to dig in. She takes the fries in her hands and stuffs them in her mouth.

"Easy, mommy," I say, reaching across the table to where Rahima's seated in her daddy's lap, taking a few of the potatoes away from her and putting them down on the napkin in front of her. Nigel and Mickey look at me and then at each other, smiling at the Kodak moment.

"So what's in the bags?" Rah asks, eyeing the Macy's bags on the floor next to my chair.

"Just a few gifts." It didn't take much for me to spend all of my tips. But I still have the money I made from doing hair last night, and my regular pay from Netta. "What size clothes does she wear?"

Rah looks down at Rahima like he can tell by eyeing her. Last night I got to know all about her: what her favorite food is, how she likes her blanket, and her ticklish spots. I changed her diaper more often than her daddy, but didn't think to check out her size. "Here, let me," I say, rising from my seat after taking another bite of my corndog and reaching over the table to gently check the tag on the back of her dress. She smiles big and initiates a peek-a-boo game, which I can't resist.

"Okay, you two. We have some serious eating to do and we're running out of time." Rah opens his arms, letting her lie across his hands and face me completely. She's the cutest little girl I've ever seen.

"She started it," I say, giggling with Rahima while her daddy fights off cracking a big smile. I know he's too happy to have his baby girl back in his life, and after paying a fertility clinic five hundred dollars yesterday, he can now prove to the courts that she belongs with him.

"Don't the three of y'all make a happy little family?" Mickey says, slurping the last of her lemonade down while Nigel eyes all of her shopping bags. She didn't find exactly what she wanted, but it looks like she got off to a good start. "Where's a camera when you need one?"

"On my cell," Nigel says, snapping a shot of us before we can protest. "I'll send it to y'all."

Rah looks down at me and then at his daughter. I know what he's thinking: Sandy will never let us happen. But Sandy's not the only one with the ability to get her hustle on to get what she wants out of life. I was doubtful about Rah's ability to take care of Kamal and Rahima. But after seeing them together, I'm convinced now that being with her daddy is the best thing for Rahima.

"Okay, it's already one-thirty. We'd better get going if we're going to be back in Compton before five." Rah has to meet Sandy at his grandparents' house at five-thirty. I know he doesn't want to give her back, but he doesn't have much choice. She's already called three times to see where he is. Rah didn't tell Sandy I was with them, but I'm sure she figured it out and isn't too pleased about it.

"Alright, man. But you need to stop by my house for a minute and get that new microphone for the sound booth if you're going to hook it up tonight," Nigel says. They're replacing some of the old studio equipment to make their demo sound even tighter. With Rah as the producer and Nigel rhyming, they make a good team. They both have their hustle and their flow in order. Unlike some other brothas I know, Nigel and Rah grow in their game, perfecting it as they move along. And that's what separates them from the rest of the crowd, which also makes them attractive to many people, including groupies.

"Alright man. We'll catch you at the crib." Mickey rubs her round belly, holding Nigel's arm securely.

We all clean up our table and head toward the escalators. We parked in different lots and will separate here. Mickey winks at me as I hold on to Rah while he's carrying his baby. Maybe Mickey's onto something with this teen romance thing.

I know it's not as easy as it looks, but maybe this family thing isn't so bad, after all. Mickey's parents have been together since high school, with many babies along the way. Maybe Rahima will bring me and Rah closer together; who knows what the future holds? At the moment, I have to give her back just like Rah does, and we both want to postpone that for as long as we possibly can.

* * *

The holiday traffic and after-church crowd make the Sunday cruise more like a crawl as we creep down Crenshaw back to Nigel's side of town. Sandy called again, wanting to know if he could bring Rahima back earlier because Sandy's got plans all of a sudden. Rah offered to keep their daughter for another night rather than rush her back, but Sandy wasn't having it and neither was Rah, who decided not to change his original plans.

I need to make a stronger repellant for him to keep Sandy away. My other one has affected Trish somewhat, but she's taking her time leaving Rah alone, too. But Sandy's a special kind of trick, and it's going to take a special kind of potion to get her off of Rah.

When we finally make it to Nigel's house, his parents aren't home from church yet. After her big lunch, Rahima fell asleep in the car. Rah managed to take her out of her car seat and put her down on Nigel's living room couch without waking her up. For a man with such big hands, Rah's touch is as light as a feather when it comes to his daughter. Rah sits down next to her, covering her with her favorite blanket.

"Jayd, tell them to be quiet before they wake up Rahima," Rah says, whispering over his daughter.

I stop at the entrance and turn around to face our friends outside. "Nigel, shhh," I whisper, causing Nigel and Mickey to look at me crazy. I look back at Rah and then out the door. We all smile at the thought of us as parents. It's a crazy picture, but nothing surprises me anymore.

Nigel leaves the front door open while he unloads Mickey's bags out of the car. She wants to look over her booty now instead of waiting until she gets home tonight. Probably because she doesn't want to hear her daddy's mouth. He could care less about the baby's wardrobe. What Mickey's father's concerned with is her marital status and so is Mickey. Her parents are serious about Mickey not being a single mother. All they need is another mouth to feed in her full house. Eyeing the joint like it's her property to scope, Mickey looks around the front yard, inspecting the five steps leading to the grand entrance, which is where I'm standing.

"What's down here?" Mickey asks, walking in and passing me by. She notices the door off to the right of the large living room. She must've seen it through the window from outside. The house has many rooms yet to be discovered. Mickey looks like she's making plans to move in. I know she has to know better than that. She met Nigel's parents and I know she can tell they aren't raising any grandbabies up in here. If she doesn't realize it, then she's in for a rude awakening.

"That's the game room. The construction's almost done. Want to see?" Nigel leads us down the six steps opening up to a large room with a massive pool table in the center. There's an air hockey table to the right, arcade games lining the back walls, and another basketball hoop attached to the to the top of the back door. They love to ball around here, no matter what kind of balling it is. Mr. Esop makes it no secret that he prefers basketball over football because he used to play pro. But as long as Nigel stays in sports, Mr. Esop's happy.

"Can you still shoot pool, Jayd?" Rah asks, leaving a sleeping Rahima on the couch and joining us. My dad has a pool table in his garage, although it's not fancy like this one. I rub my hands across the shiny red wood. It's the smoothest cherry I've ever felt and is accompanied by equally stunning, brand new balls and cues. Nigel's folks are still in the process of remodeling, but this room is pretty close to being finished.

"A little," I say, dummying down my skills. My daddy always taught me that a true hustler doesn't let his or her opponent know their true talent until they're ready to win. And we've had such a good day I don't want to ruin it by squashing Rah and Nigel's precious egos. However, I wouldn't mind kicking Mickey's ass in a game of pool. "Mickey, you play?"

"Hell nah, girl. What I look like shooting pool with these nails?" Mickey holds up her acrylic claws, showing off her fresh airbrush for me to see. I hope she knows those things will have to be toned down to wipe her baby's ass on the regular. My girl's in for a shock when her baby finally pops out. No more three-inch nails with fancy hoops hanging out of them and shit like that. She may have to settle for home manicures like mine.

"Now Mickey, if I didn't know any better, I'd say you was trying to hustle someone into thinking you're inexperienced at this game," Mr. Esop says, calling Mickey out without even knowing how true his words are. He enters through the back door of the spacious room, taking us all by surprise. His six-foot-nine frame fills up the room, immediately making my short self feel even smaller. His wife stops outside the back door, looking for something and leaving her husband to greet us first. "Hey kids."

"Hi, Mr. Esop," we all chime in unison. Mickey looks uncomfortable, but continues to stand next to Nigel at the opposite end of the table.

"Hey, Dad. How was church?" Nigel asks, picking up one of the two cue sticks lying on the felt table and passing it to Mickey, who's pleased with the attention. From the smile on Mr. Esop's face, he looks pleased with his son's latest girl. Apparently he doesn't know Mickey's about to make him a grandfather. I'm guessing his smile will turn upside down when he does find out.

"It was fine, but you'd know that if you'd come with us. You should come too, Mickey. Our church has one of the largest congregation in the entire county and we love getting visitors." The Esops belong to one of those large Black churches that come on television Sunday nights begging for more money. I never understand why those churches need so much cheddar. The Esops' church not only has a main sanctuary, but it also has a dome for their televised services, as well as an amphitheater for concerts, and other smaller buildings around the property, too. They're founding members and never miss a Sunday service.

"Thank you, Mr. Esop. I'll consider it," she says, shocking the hell out of us all, Nigel included. Mickey's really trying to get in good with his family, even pretending to be interested in the Lord when we all know she's more closely related to his nemesis—and most of the time, she's proud of it. Mickey's about as Christian as bin Laden. But if going to church means being in the family, Mickey will probably be singing in the choir before it's all said and done.

"You've got a good one here, son. You better hold on to her," Mr. Esop says, picking up a cue of his own and shooting three solid balls into a corner pocket, just for the fun of it.

"I plan on it, Dad."

Rah and I roll our eyes at each other, sick of the gushy love between our friends. I miss having Nellie and Chance around to add some comic relief to our crew. Although if she were here now, Nellie would be so jealous she wouldn't be able to contain her hating for one second, which wouldn't be funny at all. I feel Nellie's beef with the way Nigel and Mickey are handling their baby business, but there's no use in worrying about what I can't control. Nellie needs to learn that lesson, and fast, or else she's going to lose Mickey's friendship permanently.

"Yeah, son. It's better to get a good girl and hold on to her now, before you get famous. The real hussies start to come out when they can smell money on you, ain't that right, Rah?"

Rah looks around the room, trying to pretend like he didn't hear the question. He doesn't want to give an answer he might regret once Nigel's parents find out about the baby.

But Mr. Esop doesn't let him off so easy, continuing to shoot the remaining balls on the table and bait Rah into a response at the same time. "Cat got your tongue, son?"

"No, sir," Rah says, clearing his throat and standing up straight against the wall where we're posted. "You're right, sir."

"You're damned right I'm right," Mr. Esop says. "These hot-ass hussies out here these days, boy I tell you. They'll pretend like they're all innocent and what not and then, bam, they've got you right in the pocket, claiming they're carrying your baby or whatever. That's how the real hustling hussies get you, sons. And they're usually the finest ones—no offense, ladies."

Mickey looks ill and I don't think it's from her morning sickness. That phase of her pregnancy's almost over anyway.

"Not all fine girls are out to get us," Nigel says, holding on to Mickey tight, reassuring her that he's got this one. Mickey still looks ill, but more secure than ever.

"Not all, but most. That's why I'm saying keep these girls around, both of you. Learn from my mistakes, boys. Before I met your mother, there were a couple of hotties that tried to catch me up, but I'm too sharp to get hustled." Mr. Esop shoots the eight ball into another corner pocket, which he calls beforehand, like a professional. "Why do you think I learned how to play pool so well? Some people think chess teaches you about life, but not out here in this game."

"Is your father boring you with his pool philosophy again, Nigel?" Mrs. Esop asks as she seemingly floats into the room, holding freshly cut flowers from her garden. I was wondering what was taking her so long to come in from outside. She removes the large yellow hat from her head, placing it on the arm of the couch before heading into the living room. Mrs. Esop's always dressed to the nines, especially on a church day.

"Nah, he's just schooling us on the street game," Nigel says, looking relieved to see his mom. Mickey looks like she's feeling better, too, now that the conversation has been interrupted, or so we think.

"Whose little precious is this?" Mrs. Esop says, leaning back into the open doorway connecting the game room and living room.

"That's my little precious," Rah says, proudly eyeing his sleeping angel with Mrs. Esop and me. We've all heard about this little girl, but none of us have ever met. "Her name's Rahima."

"Oh Rah, she's perfect, even if you are way too young to be someone's daddy." Before we can adjust to the low blow, Mrs. Esop spots Mickey's bags by the front door. At first glance, she doesn't seem to connect all of the dots. But the shadow slowly moving across her caramel complexion and erasing her smile says that Mrs. Esop's processing all of the information.

Noticing the vibe, Mickey tries to do damage control before it all clicks for Nigel's mom. "Nigel, we'd better get going. Let me get my stuff out of your doorway," Mickey says, walking across the room toward the front door, ready to claim her goods and get going.

But not before we all have to face Mrs. Esop's interrogation.

"I can understand the baby clothes because there's a baby in the room, but are those maternity clothes in that bag? Jayd, are you pregnant?"

Why does she assume I'm the one who's pregnant? Back when I used to hang with Sandy, Mrs. Esop thought I'd gone to the bad side, becoming a hottie. But it was Rah, not me, and I thought she understood that. But, as usual, it's the girl who has to take the rap.

"No, Mrs. Esop, I'm not pregnant." Rah looks down at me, shaking his head from side to side. We both know we're all about to catch hell for our two friends.

Mickey decides to continue heading for the door, picking up one of her bags. Mrs. Esop gently but very firmly takes the light blue shopping bag away from Mickey, who was using it to hide her baby bump, which is now apparent for everyone to see. If Mickey would stop wearing her tight-ass clothes, she wouldn't look so obvious this early in the pregnancy. But it's too late to change now.

"Well, I guess now's as good a time as any to tell y'all that Mickey and I are having a baby," Nigel says, joining his girl in front of his mother. Both of his parents look too shocked to speak. But his mother's not done quite yet. Mr. Esop shakes his head as he replaces the cue stick in its holder on the wall before joining his wife in the foyer with the rest of us. Rah walks over to Rahima, who's waking up from her peaceful nap.

"I had to fight many a hussy off your father in our day," Nigel's mom says, holding her husband's arm tightly with her right hand while unconsciously crushing the flowers in her left. I can tell she wasn't, and still isn't, a woman to be messed with. Her pristine nature keeps her heat in check, but she's from Compton just like the rest of us. So I know that through her ivory Dolce & Gabbana suit and heels, she's got that ghetto girl buried deep down inside.

"Why couldn't you be more like that KJ boy I'm always hearing about? You should've played basketball this season, too. Maybe then you wouldn't have had so much idle time on your hands."

Nigel looks deflated. His dad's always riding his ass and likes to use bible scriptures to do it.

"Not to hate on KJ, but I used to date him and he's not all

that." Mr. and Mrs. Esop look at me like I just farted loudly and tried to play it off. I decide to take myself out of this conversation and join Rah in the living room.

"Yes, that's it. You need to get back into the church," his mother says, looking hard at me.

What did I do? I didn't give it up to him. That was all Mickey's doing.

"That's a good idea. First thing tomorrow morning we're going to sign you up for some extracurricular activities in the church. We'll talk to the pastor after this evening's service, which you will be attending."

Nigel looks like he just got the wind kicked out of him. "Mom, church isn't going to help and I'm not going. Me and Mickey have plans."

"The hell you do," Mrs. Esop says, claiming her son's arm and snatching him out of Mickey's clutches.

Oh shit, it's about to go down now.

"Mrs. Esop, with all due respect, me being pregnant isn't the worst thing for Nigel." Mickey looks at Nigel standing with his parents and realize she's got a battle on her hands.

I told her it wasn't going to be easy.

Mrs. Esop looks at Nigel. "We moved you out of that neighborhood so you wouldn't get caught up. But somehow you managed to anyway." She sobs into her husband's shoulder, making the horrible scene even that much more dramatic.

"Hustlers, all of them. I'm so disappointed in you, son." Even Mr. Esop's joined the bandwagon.

Just when I can't take any more, Rah comes to the rescue. "Let's bounce, Jayd. Can you get Rahima for me? I'll get her diaper bag out of the game room."

I walk over to where his daughter's playing and gently swoop her up into my arms.

"*You're getting pretty good at that, little mama,*" my mom says, invading the moment. I don't want her in my

thoughts right now. I have to concentrate on getting out of
this ugly scene. Rah signals for me to make a move toward
the door and I'm right behind him.

*"Well, next time you don't want me in your head, don't
think silly thoughts. Take for example you wishing that little
girl was yours,"* my mom says, taking the thought right out
of my head. It was only for a split second, but it was there.
Damn, she's got skills. Too bad she didn't stay in the game.
We could've used her against Esmeralda.

*"Mom, that was a fleeting thought, nothing more. You
know I don't want any babies right now. I'll talk to you
later."* I think back and I can feel her presence dissipate.

Rah looks at me quizzically, wondering what I'm thinking.
Then he smiles slightly and gives me a look of recognition:
he knows it's got something to do with my spiritual side. He
shakes his head from side to side while opening the car door
for us. It isn't a bad picture, us being a family. But, as usual,
I've spoken way too soon.

"Mom, I need to take Mickey home," Nigel says, leaving
his distraught parents standing in the doorway and escorting
Mickey to his car. I guess they've gotten bolder with their relationship if he's picking her up from home now.

Before we can escape, a car slowly rolls in front of Nigel's
house, blocking in the driveway.

"Rah, what the hell is that witch doing with my child?"
Sandy says, creeping up in her new man's car.

What did she do, track his ass down with GPS?

"Ah damn," Rah says, taking Rahima from my arms before
Sandy can get out of the car and do it herself.

I'd think Sandy wouldn't want to start something in front
of her daughter, but she doesn't look like she cares too much
about her daughter seeing her get live. I'm going to stay out
of this and let Rah handle his baby-mama bull.

"Rah, I know you hear me talking to you," she says, getting out of the car and approaching Rah's Acura. Mickey and Nigel close their car doors, ready to make an exit of their own, but Nigel's parents walk over to his car.

Now, ain't this some shit?

"Sandy, keep your voice down. This ain't your hood," Rah says, fully aware of the ghetto scene they are creating.

Nigel's parents look disgusted and victorious in their self-righteous, judgmental attitude toward us folks who still love being from the hood.

"Ra-Ra, come on, baby. It's time to go," Sandy says, snatching her daughter's arm from a vexed Rah. Rahima looks up at her daddy and starts to scream like someone's murdering her.

"Sandy, what the hell is wrong with you?" Rah says, trying to keep his voice down for the sake of their daughter, but it's impossible. Sandy's determined to show her ass today, damn the consequences.

"What's wrong with me? What's wrong with *you*?" Sandy says, successfully taking Rahima away from her daddy and getting into the car with her mute dude. "It's Ra-Ra or Jayd, Rah. You can't have them both."

Rah looks at me, defeated and embarrassed. Mr. and Mrs. Esop look at the scene with their noses up so high in the air I can read their minds.

Sandy's man's car speeds off down the block and all we can do is watch.

"These types of situations don't become us, Nigel." Mrs. Esop looks up at her husband and speaks in a monotone. "Talk to your son." She then looks down at Mickey and then at Nigel. "We'll see you at church this evening." She goes back into the house, followed by her husband. Mr. Esop looks perplexed and I can feel his confusion. But Nigel just looks ticked off, and so does Rah. How did such a cool afternoon turn into a horrific evening?

Rah's vexed about Sandy, Nigel about his parents, and all of us are powerless. Well, not all of us. When I get home, I'll try to find something in the spirit book to help us out of this tangled web we've all played a part in weaving. I still don't see how any of this is my fault, but I feel guilty and bad because my friends are going through it and I'm too emotionally beat to help them much. All I want to do is sleep this afternoon off and that's exactly what I plan on doing when I get back to Mama's house. I'll leave the spirit work for another day.

~ 10 ~
Sleepwalking

*"Wide awake in a dream/
I'm looking at you."*

—BARRY BIGGS

"Jayd, I'm going to kill her," Rah says through my cell. He just dropped me off after a silent ride home. And now he wants to talk about what happened a little while ago with Sandy at Nigel's house. I don't blame him for wanting to get rid of Sandy, but murder isn't the answer.

"That wouldn't be a very nice Christmas present for your daughter." Or maybe it would be. I just know Rah shouldn't be the one to wrap a bow round that gift. As many enemies as Sandy's made, it's just a matter of time before someone jacks her ass up. Sandy's trifling, plain and simple. I think we are all better off without her around, Rahima included. But there's got to be a better way to deal with it than violence.

"My dad used to say some people are worth more dead than alive." Rah pauses. I can hear his heavy breathing through the phone. I wish I could see his face and hold his hand as tears of anger fall from his ebony eyelashes. I've only seen Rah cry twice in his life: when his daddy got locked up and when he realized Sandy had left with his baby. "I know what he meant by that now."

"Okay, I think you've completely lost it. You know better than to say shit like that over the phone. The man is listening." I know Rah's not in the mood for jokes, but I had to deliver that one. He's not feeling me right now because I could usually get a smile or a chuckle out of him. I hate feeling Rah in so much pain. I feel for Nigel too, because, from the way his mother looked at Mickey today, he's going to be feeling Rah's anguish soon himself.

"Jayd, I'm serious. What am I going to do about this girl?"

"Honestly, I don't know, Rah. But if I've learned anything from playing Lady Macbeth for the past few weeks, it's that murder's never the answer. She lost her damned mind when she plotted to kill the king, for real. I don't want to see you sleepwalking like a crazy person." Rah laughs at my rationale, but still can't let the subject of Sandy go. At least I managed a small laugh out of him, momentarily. But he's still talking about Sandy and, as a good friend, I have to listen.

"I know. I'm not going to hurt her. But I have to get Rahima away from her. I don't want her to end up crazy like her mama." Now *that* would be a real tragedy. I step into the kitchen to find bags of Popeye's chicken and biscuits on the table. I don't know who decided to play Santa Claus, but I'm grateful for the Christmas spirit. I grab a two-piece with potato wedges and green beans and head back to Mama's room.

"Yeah, she's a sweet little girl. I pray she's too young to remember any of this shit."

I take my bags of food and clothes to Mama's room, ready to eat and catch up on our weekends, only to find that she's not in here. She must be working late at the shelter. It's after six and I hope she'll be home soon. Mama doesn't need to overexert herself. Noticing the open bathroom door across the hall, I decide to seize the opportunity and take a bath while the bathroom's free. I can warm my food up and eat afterwards.

"Me too, Jayd. Me too."

If I could melt all of Rah's baby-mama issues away, I

would. But right now I'm going to concentrate on melting away my own problems in a nice, hot bubble bath. I put my food down on the large dresser next to the bedroom door and pick up a bottle of Mama's bubble bath. She usually gives me a beauty package for Christmas with all of her best products in it. I hope some of this lavender, orange, and honey bubble bath is in my basket this year, along with this large mango candle she recently made. This will really help me relax.

"All I can say is be patient, Rah. Things will turn around. I promise."

"How can you be so sure?"

Good question. I don't know how I know it'll all work out, but I know Rahima will be with her daddy soon. Rahima's presence has changed Rah and that alone is worth fighting for her to be with him on a more regular basis.

As I watch the running water merge with the golden, fragrant liquid and create soft clouds of bubbles in the tub, I realize how the smallest addition can completely change the scenery. Before I lit the candle and poured Mama's bubble bath, creating a soothing experience, this bathroom was dull and dingy. I believe the same thing can happen with Rah's situation. It's ugly now, but with the right tools, the situation can completely transform for the better.

"I have faith, Rah. Life can't be shitty always. There has to be light at the end of the tunnel. Otherwise, why are we here?"

"You got all of that from me asking what to do about Sandy?" he says.

I can hear Rah smiling through the phone. I'd rather hear that than hear him crying any day.

"Yes and no. Let's just say life's simpler than you think." I turn the water off and walk back into the bedroom to return the bottle to its place and retrieve my bath towel, wash cloth, and robe hanging on the back of the door. "Now I hate to rush you off of the phone, but my bath awaits."

"Okay, I feel you. I'm glad you have enough faith for both of us. Sometimes I don't know," he says, taking a deep breath like my grandfather does when he talks about his days in the war.

"What don't you know?"

"I don't know what I'd do without you here to balance me. You make everything seem possible. When you were gone, everything was at a standstill."

I'm not used to Rah being so open with his feelings. I'm almost speechless, but then I remember who I'm talking to. I always have a response to my boy.

"As flattering as that is, I know your world doesn't revolve around little ole me."

"I didn't say it did, smartass. But there is something about you that keeps it moving. You know what I mean?"

I know exactly what he means. My world got dark without Rah in it. I felt like I was simply going through the motions, not really awake. Now, my whole life has changed in a matter of months and it's largely because I have Rah back in my life as a friend—and as more than that.

"Yeah, I feel you, baby," I say, running my fingers through the warm water. "Now let me go, Rah. My water's getting cold."

"Alright. And Jayd, I want you to know I was lost when you stopped talking to me, girl. I felt like I was living in a dream world without you and Rahima. And now that I've got both of you back in my life, I'm never letting go of either one of my girls again. I guess what I'm trying to say is, thank you for being here."

"Where else would I be?" It's strange how fate has a way of bringing you to a point in time no matter how many times you may have tried to avoid it.

"Well, I can think of at least one other place."

At the allusion to Jeremy, my phone beeps, indicating a call from the boy himself. I'm not taking Jeremy's call and I'm ending this one with Rah.

"Don't worry about all that," I say, locking the bathroom door and turning out the dim light above the medicine cabinet. It's time for me to chill and wash the drama of the day off. I don't want it to weigh me down, which is also what Rah needs to do. "You know, you should come by the shop and get your head done. You need a cleansing."

"You do my hair just fine."

"Yeah, but Netta can clear it. I don't want you to be distracted by things you can't control, like who I kick it with. All of your ashe needs to be focused on Rahima's best interests."

"You sound just like your grandmother, you know that?"

"Now that's the sweetest thing you've said to me all day. Night night, Rah."

"Night night, queen."

After I hung up with Rah, I finally got to take my hot bath. After which I promptly devoured my chicken, biscuits and side orders before heading to the dining room to focus on my schoolwork. I got some studying done for government class and put my English portfolio in order in preparation for our AP meetings on Wednesday. Now that I've finished my schoolwork for the evening, I can finally get into bed. I pack up my backpack and set it on the floor next to the table.

The small charm bag Mama gave me for my first day of school is still hanging on the side of my bag, along with the keychain picture of me and my crew from the Masquerade Ball. I hope we can get it together before this picture is irrelevant. Feeling drained, I return to the bedroom I share with Mama, and lay my head back on my pillow, pull my covers over my body, and melt into my bed, ready for a good night's sleep. Right before I drift off completely, my phone rings, making me jump. Why is my father calling so late and interrupting my flow?

"Hey, Daddy," I say, answering the phone on the first ring. I know I forgot to call him and set up the dates for my driving lessons and I don't want him to think I've lost interest.

"Hey, girl. You still too busy to call your old man, I see," he says, not letting me off the hook for a minute. "But I still managed to book your lessons for this week. Is that good for you, Miss Jackson?"

"Yes, Mr. Jackson. I appreciate it greatly." Sometimes I can joke with my daddy, but unfortunately our relationship is full of the tension that predates my existence on earth. With him, my guard is always up.

"So, they'll pick you up after school every day this coming week. Your lessons are for an hour a day. I told them to meet you at the front office. If you want to change, just give them a call. You ready to write down the information?"

"I'm actually sleeping now. Can you call back and leave it on my voice mail please?" I sweetly request, but I know that pissed him off. He says I'm too spoiled by my grandmother as it is and that I remind him too much of my mother. No wonder I'm not nicer to him.

"Jayd, I'm doing all of this for you and you can't even get up to write the information down? Boy, I tell you," he says.

Mama's still not home from the shelter and it's almost eleven. I think Bryan's picking her up after work. Hopefully, I'll be asleep by the time they get in.

"Okay, Daddy, I'm up," I say, searching for my backpack at the foot of my bed, only to find I've left it in the dining room. I get up and turn the light switch on the wall and open the door, feeling the warm blast from the heater on the floor. I walk through the living room to quickly retrieve my bag and get back into Mama's room and take out the small datebook in my backpack to take down the information. I'm only wear-

ing my nightshirt and scarf—no robe or slippers on my feet.
If Mama's saw me outside of my bed like this, she'd have a
conniption.

"Okay, the name of the school is Better by the Beach Driver's
Training. The name of your instructor is Tina and she'll be
there tomorrow at three." I write it all down.

"Thank you, Daddy. Tell Faye I said hi." If it weren't for my
stepmother, we probably wouldn't talk as much as we do,
even if it is limited. She's pretty cool most of the time. But,
like everyone, she has her good days and her bad ones.

"Will do. And I'll see you for the family Christmas dinner.
Don't forget and let me know in advance if you need a ride,"
he says.

He knows I'm going to need one unless Rah can take me.
But I'll wait and see how the week unfolds. "Okay, Daddy.
See you then." I hang up the phone and put it down on the
dining room table.

I put up the datebook and set my backpack down on the
dining room chair, eyeing the five books and several single-
subject notebooks inside. I have a ton of work to do before
the holiday's up. Now maybe I can get some rest. It's been a
long, emotional day and I have a long, emotional week
ahead of me. I know Laura's going to try her best to take my
role from me. And with Mrs. Bennett by her side she can
probably get away with it, or so she thinks.

I'm going to work on polishing my paper on Queen Califia and study my spirit lessons at the same time. I know my
ancestors had way more drama to get through than this. If
anything can help me see my path clearly, it'll be my spirit
lessons or the contents of the spirit book at home. I'll take a
look at my mom's notebook tomorrow and then study in the
spirit room when I get home tomorrow. Until then, sleep will
have to be my savior.

*   *   *

"Out damned spot, out I say!" I'm on stage as Lady Mac-
beth's crazy ass, sleepwalking through the castle. I love this
scene because I can feel her guilt about her part in the mur-
der of the king. But it's not my character's pain I'm experi-
encing in the moment: it's my own.

"Out damned spot! What was that?" I walk over toward
the audience, which looks sparse in the black background.
A girl's hand reaches out of the darkness and grabs my
hand. It's Laura, pulling me down into the audience.

"Sit down," she whispers harshly in my face, pulling me
out of character. "You don't belong here." She stands up,
shouting in the quiet theater. "Give me my crown!" Laura
pulls my arm hard, forcing me to lose my footing and fall
into the front row of the audience. While I'm down, Laura
snatches the jewel-encrusted tiara off my head, pulling my
hair in the process.

"Ouch!" I scream, reaching up and returning the favor.

Laura grabs my hand and we fight for the queen's crown.
The crowd around us clears the path to let the brawl ensue.
I can see Mrs. Bennett's evil smile in the background, but no
one's face becomes clear. It's just me and Laura and my
crown. After a few moments of intense struggling, Reid, also
in character as Macbeth, appears behind Laura.

"If we should fail?" Reid asks, completely in character.
Before I can deliver my response, Laura takes the words
right out of my mouth.

"We fail! But screw your courage to the sticking-place,
and we'll not fail."

Even though Laura's acting like she's in character, the look
in her eyes tells me she's talking about something else com-
pletely and Reid, being under her spell, doesn't even get it.

"Jayd, your cell is out here. Do you want to lose it or
what?" Jay says, cracking open the bedroom door and waking

me up with my ringing phone. I neglected to buy batteries for my classic Tasmanian Devil alarm clock and set my phone alarm last night when I got off the phone with my dad.

"Thank you, Jay." He saved me from losing my phone to one of my thieving uncles, and I am grateful. It's the holidays and I know they'd be tempted to pawn my shit in exchange for a couple of bucks. The sad fact is that it doesn't have to be the holidays for my uncles to jack: it's their main hustle all year long.

"Whatever. Keep up with your stuff so I don't have to wake up to turn it off. Brothas need beauty sleep, too." Jay tosses my phone on the foot of my bed and goes back to his top bunk in Daddy's room for another hour of sleep. At least he gets his rest. I have to get up before sunrise after dealing with crazy-ass dreams.

I'm going to have to seriously look into support groups for other children born with cauls. Too bad I won't have much support for my day today. I can only imagine what Mrs. Bennett has in store for me. She couldn't get to me on Friday because the principal was out, even though she made me stay in the office and miss my first dress rehearsal.

I'm going to go through my day like nothing's happened, like it was all a bad dream. Maybe if I act innocent then nothing will happen to me. Owning a guilty conscience is what got Lady Macbeth caught up. And if my dream is any indication of what's to come—and I know it is—Laura's going to fight hard for my part and I'm not giving in that easily.

Monday wasn't as eventful as I had anticipated. My entire crew was absent from school today. I didn't expect to see Nigel or Mickey today after yesterday's tumultuous encounter with Nigel's parents. But Nellie and Chance being absent is interesting. Jeremy's attendance is always a crapshoot, especially when it's a gorgeous, windy day making for good surf, like today.

With the various school activities going on before the holidays, the administration is holding meetings for two days, keeping even Mrs. Bennett too busy to torture me. But I'm sure by Wednesday she'll be back on my ass. Until then, I'm going to get my study and rehearsal on like never before. Even Laura's chilled out, making our rehearsal more tolerable than usual. I guess Mickey was right. Without my confession, they've got nothing on me, no matter what letter they think they may have.

Now, riding around in this rickety Nissan Sentra with this hippie lovechild showing me the difference between the gas and the brake, I'm missing my crew being together more than ever. I didn't tell Rah or Mickey about my lessons because they have other things to worry about. Also, if I don't do well I don't want anyone to know. But I do know this chick is wasting my time, like I don't know the parts of a car. But I guess she's just doing her job.

"Okay, Jayd. That ends your first lesson. Tomorrow you will drive. Sound good?" my instructor says, pulling up to Miracle Market, our designated drop-off spot. I didn't want her taking me home for fear of being teased by my hood folks, family included. I also don't want to remind Mama that I'm taking lessons my daddy's paying for.

Ain't that some backwards shit, having to hide the fact that my father is paying for me to have something? But that's how it is and I have to play the hand I've been dealt, no matter how unfair it may seem.

Tuesday went by without so much as a peep from anyone. When Nigel and Mickey finally arrived at school, they were summoned to the office and spent the entire day there. Mrs. Bennett didn't come to rehearsal either. I'm guessing both are related, but I'm trying not to think about that situation at all. My rehearsals have been going well, even if my dress didn't fit. It was about four inches too long and has to be taken up at the hem and let out in the arms. As long as it's ready for Monday night's opening, it's all good.

"Jayd, this is for you," Mrs. Peterson says as soon as I set foot in her class. I had an AP meeting for break and it was basically an extension of English class with our English teacher, Mrs. Malone, taking over for Mrs. Bennett, who wasn't there. It's been so nice not seeing the wench on a regular basis that I almost forgot what she looks like.

"Can I leave my books here?" I ask, reading the summons to the attendance office. I get a chill up my arm from holding the small yellow note that lets me know this isn't good. The look in Mrs. Peterson's eyes confirms my intuition.

"I don't think you'll be back," she says with a smile while looking down at her newspaper.

What's really going on?

"Hey Jayd," Jeremy says, entering the classroom as I exit. "Aren't you going the wrong way?"

"Apparently not. My presence has been requested in the office." I show Jeremy the slip and he shakes his head from side to side. I know he's seen many of these in his days here. Me, I've only seen one and this second occurrence is not welcome.

"Good luck. I hope it's not too serious. Whatever you do, don't let them see you sweat," he says, like I'm about to go into a boxing ring. "They can smell fear on their opponent."

"Thanks for the advice, Don King."

Jeremy laughs and gives me a hug. The bell rings above our heads. Other students rush past us into the classroom, but we don't move. His arms are so warm and he smells like Irish Spring. I'm glad I ran into him before going to face these folks in the front. I'll be so relaxed from Jeremy's energy that they won't be able to upset me too bad, I hope.

"I'll call you later." Jeremy watches me walk off toward the main office. For once, I'm going to miss being in government class.

When I make it to the attendance office, Mrs. Bennett is waiting for me outside.

"Jayd, so glad you could make it. Come right in," she says, opening the door to the assistant principal's office. I've never been in here before, but it's just as dull as the rest of the offices up here.

When I step inside, I notice Mickey and Nigel sitting in two seats across from the desk, which is located in the center of the room. Mrs. Bennett escorts me to another chair next to the desk on the opposite side. I sit, and she sits down in the chair next to mine.

"Mr. Brown will return momentarily," she says. I look at my friends, who both look a wreck. I haven't spoken to either of them since Sunday and I'm completely out of the loop.

"Ah, this must be the infamous Jayd Jackson," Mr. Brown says. I recognize him from school assemblies, but we've never met. He walks past us and takes a seat behind the large desk. In his hands are several files, and I'm assuming that one of them is mine.

Here we go.

"Mr. Brown, the letter in question is in the red folder," Mrs. Bennett says, pointing to one of the files in his hand.

"Ah, yes. Thank you. Now, Miss Jackson, we're really not all that concerned with your role in this serious infraction of school policy, which is apparently a repeated violation for your friend Mickey here," he says, eyeing another folder.

"But we do know that you played a role, indeed," Mrs. Bennett snarls.

Where does she get off acting like she's the almighty?

"Yes, well, see, that's why you're here. We've yet to determine who forged the signature or whether or not the note is indeed forged. That's why we need you to tell us the truth, young lady." Mr. Brown looks at me in such a paternalistic way I want to get up and smack him in the face. He's not my daddy and he shouldn't assume shit about me, even if he is right. I didn't want to help Mickey ditch in the first place and I'm pissed as ever to be sitting in the office, wasting my time. So he's got it all wrong if he thinks I wanted to help them out.

"What he's saying, Jayd, is that you can save us a full investigation by simply confessing right now. That way, you'd be able to negotiate keeping your part in the play and suspending your punishment until after the holiday. But if you don't confess, well, then we'll have no choice but to put you on immediate probation while we investigate your role in this matter, which will also mean the immediate surrender of your lead." Mrs. Bennett looks like she's just won a million dollars as she serves me my cold portion of her bitch's brew.

"I don't understand," I say, ready to feign ignorance. I'm not letting them entrap me into a confession. I don't know what Mickey and Nigel said to them, but I know they didn't rat me out. Unlike Nellie, they've got more loyalty to the unspoken code between friends than she does. "If you don't know for a fact the letter in question is a forgery, then why are we here?"

"Look, young lady, you're in enough trouble as it is without all the sass. Backtalk won't do anything but land you in more hot water." Mr. Brown turns red as he talks to me. I guess Mrs. Bennett's already filled him in on her opinion of my attitude.

"And to answer your question, you're in here because we have an eye witness who says you signed the letter in his or her presence."

She can generalize the pronoun all she wants. I know it was a she. Which she—Laura, Nellie or Misty—is the question.

"Well, if you want to do this the hard way, so be it. But I think it's very selfish of you to let down your fellow thespians. Now your understudy will have to play your part." Mrs. Bennett looks victorious as she snatches away my part in the blink of an eye.

Mickey and Nigel look sorry and I know that they are. But that doesn't make me feel any better. How am I going to explain this to my cast and, more importantly, to Mama?

"That's all for now, Jayd. Thank you," Mr. Brown says, writing me a pass to return to class.

What the hell?

"When we return from the winter break, we'll launch a full investigation to get to the bottom of this matter. I don't think you all realize how serious this is." Mr. Brown looks at me sternly and then to a beaming Mrs. Bennett. I have a feeling he's trying to impress her. He then returns his gaze to me and smiles. "Have a good holiday, Miss Jackson."

And without another word, Mrs. Bennett rises from her chair and opens his office door, waiting for my departure.

Damn, these fools up here are cold. But like Jeremy advised, I'm not going to let them see me sweat or cry. I'm going to wait until I'm outside before showing my emotions.

Mrs. Peterson's not expecting me back, so I decide to sit in the courtyard where the seniors and cozy couples hang out during the breaks. No one's here right now and I need the quiet to wrap my head around the last few weeks. I place my backpack on my lap and hug it tightly, again noticing my charm bag with the word "listen" written across the front. This bag saved me from getting into a fight with KJ's ex-trick. Maybe it'll help me see my way through this mess.

"Jayd, are you okay?" Ms. Toni says, catching me by surprise. She joins me on the cozy bench, placing her file folders on her lap and putting her left arm around my shoulder, causing the tears puddling in my eyes to break away from their safety net and slide down my cheek. I can't stop thinking about how many ways I could've played this scenario out differently.

"Not really," I say, wiping the tears from my cheeks with the back of my sweatshirt sleeve. It's a chilly day and I'm still in need of a real coat. Ms. Toni's thin frame doesn't help to warm me up and the smell of her cigarettes is all over her jacket, making me back up little. "Mickey and Nigel got busted ditching and the administration thinks they can prove that I forged Mickey's note to return to school."

"Oh Jayd," Ms. Toni says, taking a deep breath. "That's not good. They could suspend you and take your part for something like that."

"They already took my part and gave it to Laura, but the full investigation won't take place until after the holiday." Saying it aloud sounds even worse than I feel. How could I be so stupid? I feel like I exist in a dream state because this can't be happening to me. Mama will have my ass in a sling if she finds out I did something this stupid.

"Please tell me you didn't do it." I look up at Ms. Toni and then back down. More tears well up in my eyes and Ms. Toni rubs my shoulder. "Girl, girl, girl."

"I know," I say, admitting my mistake without giving up the full confession. Ms. Toni's cool and all, but she's still a teacher. I can only reveal so much information to her without putting us both in compromising positions. I know she'd do anything for me, but even she's no match for this lily-white administration, as we've seen before.

"You'll be okay, Jayd. Just learn your lesson this time around. Mrs. Bennett doesn't need bullets when you give her all the ammunition she needs to take you down. And Laura—well, let's just say I've known her and Reid for a long time and they are just as bad as Mrs. Bennett when it comes to seeking revenge." Ms. Toni looks across the courtyard toward the entrance to the main hall and smiles. I follow her gaze and smile myself at the sight of the fine brotha walking into our public confessional.

Mr. Adewale walks over to where we're seated. "Hello," he says, standing over us both. "I've been trying to catch up with you, young lady. I found some more information on Queen Califia." Noticing the sullen vibe, Mr. A crosses his arms across his chest, waiting to be filled in on the grim news. "So, who died?"

"The first Black Lady Macbeth at South Bay High." He looks at me sternly and shakes his head from side to side. The bell rings, signaling the end of third period. The last thing I want to do is sit in math class, but I guess I have no choice in the matter.

"I'll see you in rehearsal, Jayd. And keep your chin up. It'll get better." Ms. Toni smiles at Mr. A before she gets up, with me following right behind her. The last thing I need is a tardy or any other reason for my name to come up in the front office.

"What's this all about?" Mr. Adewale follows me out of the courtyard, joining the oncoming traffic of bodies rushing to fourth period.

"I lost my part because Mrs. Bennett thinks she has some note proving my part in helping Mickey and Nigel ditch. I know, I'm stupid and I let everyone down. Go ahead, say I told you so."

But Mr. Adewale does nothing of the sort. Instead, he stops me in my tracks and looks at me intensely. I almost feel like he's probing my mind or something, he's looking at me so intently. If I didn't know better, I'd swear time has momentarily stopped and we are the only two people moving.

"Whatever you do, Jayd, don't admit to something you didn't do. But if you did do it, then tell the truth when presented with proof: you'll have more power in it. If there's no proof, say nothing. Let them think what they want, but keep your mouth shut. I know that'll be a new one for you, but true hustlers don't show their hands."

After his exposé, Mr. A winks at me and walks off, leaving me in the main hall to wonder what the hell that was all about. Again, my charm bag hits me in the hip, making me notice the word "listen." All I want to do is end this day, damn the advice.

I've been in a funk all afternoon because of all of my drama at school. I can't even enjoy my driving lessons and this blonde chick is working my nerves. I wish I could drive straight to Compton, dropping her off somewhere before I get home. But I only have three more lessons and, if I don't blow it, I could have my license before Christmas. I may be offtrack at school, but my personal goals are still on the money.

"Please make a left here," Tina instructs.

All we've done in the two days she's been teaching me is drive to the beach and back. She gets out and shops a little while I practice parking with my hazard lights on. Tina even had the nerve to stretch out for twenty minutes because the sun crept out of the clouds for a little while. I stayed in the car because I'm never dressed for the beach. And I hate this little cheap-ass Nissan Sentra. I'd never buy this car. Every time we go over a bump in the road, I feel like the entire car's going to fall apart.

"Here, as in this corner, or here, as in the stop sign up ahead?" Tina's very indirect with her instructions and I don't think that's a good thing when it comes to driving.

"Here, as in right here, at *this* corner," she says, pointing her yellow pencil out of the window to make her point more clear. "Uh oh, Jayd. You didn't use your blinker to indicate your traffic movement. I'm going to have to dock you for that." She marks yet another check on the long sheet. I forgot about the quiz today and it couldn't have come at a more difficult time. I can barely focus on the road ahead, let alone concentrate on her vague directions.

"Now please find a spot and parallel park." Tina looks down at the sheet, ready to mark it up.

"Parallel park? You never taught me how to do that."

"Well, Jayd, you've been studying your textbook, right? Just try it anyway. It's a practice test. The one that counts is on Friday."

As I pull up next to a parked car on the small street across from my high school, I notice Nellie, Laura and Reid walking up the walkway with a stack of papers and Nellie with a stapler in her hand.

Laura takes her staple remover and rips the Fall Festival fliers off of the bulletin board in front of the main office. She then takes one of the papers from Nellie's stack and staples it in place of the old paper, promptly tossing the latter into the garbage bag Reid's holding.

"Jayd, wake up. Did you fall asleep while driving? That's a definite no-no." Tina jots down yet another note and I really couldn't care less.

"I'm sorry. What did you say?"

Tina looks at me, closes her notebook and taps it her with her pencil. She purses her thin, pink lips together, wishing she could cuss me out and I know the feeling. But neither one of us wants to go there. I want my license and she wants to get paid. As long as we each concentrate on our independent goals, we'll be fine.

"Okay, Jayd, let's start heading home. You don't seem into this lesson at all. Pull out and make a right turn at the light."

Without looking over my shoulder, I pull out onto the

small street, not realizing a car's coming. Seeing Reid, Laura and Nellie take down the signs with my name on them and putting up new ones with Laura's name as Lady Macbeth was too much for me to swallow.

"Jayd, watch out!" Tina shouts, pulling up the emergency break and stopping me from hitting the car just in time. "Jayd, snap out of it before you kill us both. Please." Tina's right, I need to wake up and snap out of this funk. There's got to be a way to change my luck. Otherwise, I'm going to hurt someone, most likely myself.

~ 11 ~
Hustler's Luck

"The weak hearted become Babylon puppets/
Making it hard for real hustlas."

—COMMON

The back door is always open. Lucky for us enough people live in this house that someone's usually home. When I get inside the gate, I walk through the back door straight to my room. I don't hear anyone in the den and as far as I know, Mama's not in the spirit room. From the looks of it, no one's here except for me, Lexi, and Jay, who's sleeping in his room. It must be nice to have such a leisurely existence.

"Come on, girl. Did anyone feed you yet?" I ask Lexi as she follows me out of the hallway and back into the kitchen. Lexi only comes in the house with Mama or me, and this is as far as she ever goes. "Let's both get a snack," I say, petting her dark gray coat. I know Mama's busy if Lexi needs a bath and a haircut. She won't let anyone bathe her dog, and Lexi won't have it any other way. I'm grateful because I know that would be one of my chores and I don't need anymore work to do.

After I feed both Lexi and myself a quick bite, I decide to take advantage of the quiet house and claim a spot on the couch. I need to get lost in my work and forget about the day I just had. Tuesday was extremely awkward after I was so cruelly relieved of my role as Lady Macbeth.

And Wednesday wasn't any better. Having to watch Laura

and Reid act like husband and wife onstage was a bit much for me to stomach today. Everyone was shocked when I came to rehearsal and sat down in the audience. But honestly, what else could I do, throw a fit and pull out her hair like I did in my dream? I'm not going out like that, especially not here. Me acting out like that would make Mrs. Bennett's entire year. Besides, we've got a few more days before opening night and anything can happen between now and then. I'm now Laura's understudy and, with any luck, she will get sick or stuck in traffic or something. I'm willing to wish almost anything up if it'll get my part back. And if there's anything that'll do the trick, it's in my spirit studies, which I'm getting into right now.

Before I can get too lost in my studies, I hear the back gate open, announcing my temporary peace is now threatened by someone else's presence in the house. By the way Lexi's tail is wagging underneath the kitchen table, it can only be one person coming through the back door: Mama.

"Jayd, how was your day?" Mama asks in a weary voice that sounds weak enough to make me worry. She's just getting in from the shelter and her ankles look swollen from being on her feet all day.

I put my notebook, pen and spirit book down to tend to my grandmother's needs. Even if she doesn't say it, I know Mama's bone-tired and needs a break. The holidays always whip her ass and I've been so wrapped up in my own crap I haven't been much of a help to her lately.

"It was cool," I say, taking her two heavy bags and placing them on the couch next to my backpack and pile of work, Mama's assignments included. I walk into our room and grab her herb satchel to make her a tonic while she takes a seat at the dining room table. She looks like she could use a few potions to reenergize her body and soul.

"I wish I could say same the same thing. Those people

down at that shelter are going to drive me crazy and run me ragged at the same time."

I walk back into the kitchen and take a large mason jar out of the cupboard. I empty the multicolored herbs into the clear jar before filling it with tap water. Mama doesn't believe in buying bottled water. She says paying for water—which comes from our mother deity Oshune—is the biggest hustle of all time and she refuses to play that game.

"Mama, haven't you warned me about letting people pimp my ashe?" I hand Mama the large concoction, ready to get back to my work. Mama looks like she's ready to take a long nap.

"Well, isn't this something new; the student advising the teacher. Now that you're working with Netta, you think you can school me, huh, little queen?" Mama smiles up at me, gulping down her herbal potion in three swift swallows. How she takes all of those bitter herbs without choking has fascinated me since I was a child. I can barely tolerate the smell while mixing them up for her.

"Never, Mama. I'm just worried about you, that's all." I take the empty glass back into the kitchen, adding it to the pile of dirty dishes occupying the sink. I don't know whose night it is to wash them but I'm not doing it. I haven't used a single dish today and I'll be damned if I get stuck with this job.

"Is that why you look like you've been through hell and back?" Mama comments, eyeing me carefully as I sit in the chair across from her, raising her small feet into my lap so I can rub them for her. Mama relaxes at my touch, but doesn't drop her questioning. "Well, are you going to tell me what's going on with you or do I have to find out on my own?" Mama's green eyes look tired, but they haven't lost a bit of their glow or their power. She probes my face for an inkling of a response. Getting what she was looking for, Mama closes her eyes and waits for me to dish.

"I lost my part in the school play," I say, leaving out the drama with Rah and Sandy. I don't want to overwhelm Mama with my problems. She's already been through enough. But if anyone can advise me on how to deal with Laura and Mrs. Bennett, it's Mama.

"Now, how did you manage to let that happen?"

Mama doesn't open her eyes, but I can tell by her response she already knows. I guess my eyes gave me away, or rather her eyes came in and got the information she needed. Mama's got vision skills like no other.

"It's a long story. But basically, I got caught up in some of Mickey and Nigel's crap and, well, the understudy's now in the lead and I'm the understudy."

"Well, Jayd, sometimes that's how the cookie crumbles," Mama says, opening her eyes and looking at her bags on the couch next to my work. "Have you been studying the 'doing hair' section of the spirit book?" She takes her feet out of my lap and gets up to retrieve the large book. "Netta will expect you to take the initiative when it comes to learning your family's lineage of doing hair. She can't teach you that part," Mama says, thumbing through the book and turning to a section in the front.

"No, I haven't gotten that far yet. I've been studying for my quiz and working on my Califia paper."

The way Mama looks at me makes me feel like a little girl making excuses to the teacher about why her homework's late, again. "Jayd, you are going to have to learn how to walk, chew bubblegum and do hair all at the same time if you're going to make it as a priestess. And, more importantly, you can't let anyone take your crown."

As the seemingly innocent words flow from Mama's

mouth, the vision of Laura snatching the crown off of my head in my dream Sunday night comes to mind.

Mama smiles at me and hands me the open book, pointing to a potion called "Hustler's Luck".

"What's this for?" I ask, reading the ingredients and the story behind it.

Mama walks back over to the couch, takes her bags and heads for her room. I know Mama's about to soak in a hot bath and go straight to bed. I guess we're on our own for dinner again. Mama hasn't cooked for the household regularly since she started working overtime at the shelter. And I don't expect that'll change too much until after the holidays are over. But she'll make up for it by cooking on Christmas Eve.

"It's to help you get back what's rightfully yours. Next time, pay more attention to the consequences of your actions, Jayd. You never know when your mistakes will come back and bite you in the ass," Mama shouts from her room. She walks across the hallway, wearing her house robe and slippers and carrying the same candle and bubble bath I used for my bath on Sunday.

"I could sure use some of this," I say. The potion appears to be an anything-goes spray, which means it can be whatever I need it to be, whenever I need it to be.

"Oh yeah, that's the one," my mom says, adding her opinion to the mix. "I remember Mama made me some of that when my watch was stolen at school. I went to school the next day and sprayed some of that all over myself before every classroom I went into until the perpetrator choked from the scent. I whipped that girl's ass until she gave me my watch back. If any potion will get you your part back, that one will do it, Jayd."

"If you make it right, you should have your part back by

opening night. It won't get rid of all of your problems, but it will help your luck turn around. And tell your mother I'm looking forward to seeing her and Karl at dinner next Thursday," Mama says before she locks herself in the bathroom.

"Mama's too much," my mother adds before exiting my thoughts and leaving me to concentrate on my good luck potion. I'll move my studying to the spirit room where I can really get into this for the rest of the night. By morning, I should have everything all figured out. We'll see who gets the standing ovation opening night. Until then, I'll lay low like Lady Macbeth and wait for my prey to come to me.

By the time I came back in the house last night, it was almost midnight and Mama was knocked out. It took me all night to get finished with my schoolwork and my spirit assignment, which I think was very successful. I'll have to wait and see how Laura reacts to the potion when I spray it this afternoon. According to the book, I can use it as a hair, body, room, and linen spray, as well as just a simple air freshener. As tired as I am this Thursday morning, I wish I could use it as a pick-me-up.

"You're up early, I see," I say to my uncle Bryan, who's already dressed. It's only five thirty-five, so I know I'm not running late this morning.

"Yeah, I'm pulling double shifts at Miracle Market so I can buy this girl a stupid Christmas gift."

"Oh yeah, my new auntie," I say to Bryan as I creep into his room, grabbing my weekend bag, which I packed last night, and my toiletries from inside the small closet. This new girlfriend of his has made Bryan a steady hair client and I'm grateful for the business. I'm not complaining, but one day I would like to know what it's like to have my own room, complete with real dresser drawers and all. I've got to tighten my money-making skills if I'm going to get what I want and need around here. "How's the hustle going?"

"As hustles go, girl. Slow and steady wins the race. You know I'll be out there Christmas Eve when folks will really need a gift. That's when we'll hike up the prices on everything and really make a dime, you feel me?"

"Yeah, it's called inflation," I say, smiling at my uncle. Out of them all, he's on his game and, as the youngest of Mama's children, he also catches the most heat from the others. But, like a champion, Bryan sends the hater rays right back at them.

"Don't hate the player, hate the game," he says, turning off the bathroom light just to mess with me. I turn the switch on the wall back on, watching him walk into the living room to heat up his body on the other side of the floor heater.

"Are you bringing my new auntie to dinner?" I ask, spreading my toiletries across the laundry hamper. I need to make a run to Target and stock up on supplies. Noticing the mess Bryan's left for me this morning, I leave the bathroom and follow him as he moves from his post by the heater into the kitchen. I need a paper towel to wipe down the sink after his trifling ass left water all over the place and, as precious as toilet paper is around here, I don't want to waste a single square.

"Maybe, maybe not," he says, eating the last of his cornflakes before putting the bowl into the sink. He must've started eating them when he first got up. "We'll see how I'm feeling that night. You know how Mama gets at Christmas. She'll have us married by Easter with grandbabies by Halloween and I'm not ready for any of that yet."

He's right about Mama. Rah's the only boy I've ever brought to any of my family gatherings and I can't shake him—permanently. Mama has her favorites and knows how to make them stick when she wants to.

"Yeah, I can feel you there. And thanks again for the mess you left me," I say sarcastically, ripping a paper towel from the holder and heading back into the bathroom before someone else slides in.

"Don't say I never gave you nothing," he says, opening the back door and dipping out, taking the last word with him.

That's okay; I'll get him later. Right now all I want to do is get to school and test my potion out. I can't wait to choke Laura up with this shit.

Mama's little pep talk last night has caused me to think about this play in a whole new light. As the understudy, no one really pays attention to my movements too much, which will allow me to work some magic of my own around the dressing room and classroom. I'm going to get my part back before opening night or my name isn't Jayd Jackson. Netta teaching me how to cleanse the shop last weekend gave me a new perspective on controlling my surroundings and I'm going to see what happens when I give the drama room a good spiritual scrub-down and replace it with some sweet-smelling energy of my own.

It's the Friday before the Fall Festival and the holiday buzz is in the air more than ever. For me, though, it's a rough day. The final rehearsal before the practice run-through is today, and as I head down to the drama room, everyone looks excited about the event. On my way, I notice Mickey and Nigel walking toward the main office.

"Hey y'all, wait up," I say, jogging over to where they are walking across the quad, careful not to let any of my potion spill out of the miniature spray container I put it in last night. I want to savor all of my golden potion and make sure it's used for its intended purpose only. I can't wait to get to the dressing room and get started on my cleansing. I even jotted down a Legba chant to say, just to add to my good luck.

"What's up, Jayd?" Nigel says.

They both apologized already for me losing my part, and I've forgiven them, for the time being. But they both know they have to do their part in fixing this mess and I'll do mine.

"My parents are coming to campus to talk with the principal about my ditching, Mickey's pregnancy, everything. This sucks big time, man."

Damn, Nigel's in for it when Mr. and Mrs. Esop get the whole story. And if they find out I helped, they'll never trust me again. It's one thing for the school to think I'm down with their ditching, put me on probation and take my part away from me. The administration already thinks badly of me, no matter how wrong they are. But for Nigel's parents to think that I intentionally set their son up to get played is another thing altogether.

"I'm sorry, baby," Mickey says, trying to console Nigel. But he looks unmoved by her attempt to comfort him.

"Everything will work out, Nigel. Don't worry."

He looks at me, noticing I no longer seem afraid of the outcome, unlike when he saw me in the main office for our interrogation Wednesday. "How can you be so sure?"

Mickey looks as comfy under Nigel's arm as I feel in my powers now. I know what my true gift is and it walks hand in hand with my hustle. "I have faith and a little something extra."

Mickey and Nigel watch the seagulls fly above our heads and off toward the beach and I follow their gaze. Students and teachers alike whiz by us as we remain still, even with the ringing bell over our heads. Lunch is officially over and, along with it, the beginning to the end of this horrific week.

"I'd better go," Nigel says somberly. "Since you have so much faith, could you say a prayer for me? My dad's threatening to send me to a private school next semester if I don't straighten up. And I don't want to switch schools again."

"Already done, son." Unlike Mickey, Nigel accepts my comfort and heads off to meet his destiny, with Mickey close by his side.

Speaking of destiny, here's Mrs. Bennett to play her role in mine as the bitterest bitch of all time.

"Jayd, it seems as if this year you are in a perpetual state of despondency. Is life treating you well?"

Hell no, everything's not okay, but I'll be damned if I let her know what I'm thinking. Why does she always have to sound like she's teaching one of our AP prep courses?

"Yes, everything's fine," I lie, resuming my trek toward the drama room. Unfortunately, that's also where she's headed. Now that I'm no longer in the lead, I don't have to be there for the lunch rehearsals. I already know the part like the back of my hand, making me the best understudy in the world. Laura's the one who needs the rehearsing. Besides, I could use the break before I steal my part back on opening night. It's going to take everything I've got plus some to take Laura down without getting caught. All I need is the perfect opportunity.

"If you need to talk to someone, you know the school has a teen help hotline," she says to my back.

Is she referring to the call-in center troubled kids use when they're desperate? I know this trick is tripping if she thinks she can affect me that deeply. I have to slow down and check her real quick before I get to her protégé.

"You don't need to worry. I'll never give you the satisfaction of committing suicide," I say. From the creases forming at the top of her already wrinkled forehead, I can tell Mrs. Bennett's not amused.

"I've known people to kill themselves over smaller things," she says, with a forlorn look in her eyes.

From the softening in her voice, I know Mrs. Bennett's not talking about me anymore. Maybe someone she knows killed him- or herself and I've hit a nerve. I didn't mean to come at her like that, but she started it.

"You're right," I say, not knowing what else to say.

Before I can sympathize too much, Mrs. Bennett regains her evil composure and refocuses her attention on me and my supposed sorrow. But I know it's just a little bad luck that needs reversing.

"Jayd, some things in life aren't meant to be, even if at first you get what you want. Recent events in your life are the perfect example of this truth," Mrs. Bennett says, now leading the way to the drama room. "First, your short-lived relationship with Jeremy and now, your lead in Macbeth. Fate, it seems, has a sense of humor," she says, walking away from the scene of her own verbal hit-and-run.

I never knew a teacher could be my worst hater ever. Now I'm more determined than ever to gain back what I have lost and I'm well on my way to doing it, if I could only get this broad out of my way.

"By the way, the core cast is rehearsing in the main theater so that the drama room can be cleaned for next week's opening. The rest of the class is meeting outside—that includes you."

She never quits, does she? I guess my cleansing will have to wait for Monday. I just hope it won't be too late for my potion to work.

It's my last day of driving lessons and I can't even be all that happy about it. After failing my pretest Wednesday, I'm slightly nervous about taking it again, especially since they report it all to my dad, being that his name's on the check. He already chewed me out about wasting his money on lessons I'm not taking seriously, and I don't want to hear his mouth again. My dad said he'd take me for my test in the morning if I'm up by seven. He knows how to ruin a sistah's Saturday, that's for sure. But I'm not going to complain if it means I get to drive.

At least I'll have a guaranteed ride to my mom's this afternoon, and I get to drive there from here. It's the first time Tina's letting me drive all the way home and so far, so good. We're only one block away from my mom's street and, from what I can tell, I don't have as many red checks on the paper as I did last time.

If all goes well, tomorrow I should be able to take my test in the morning and drive to the cast party tomorrow night, if my mom lets me borrow her car. Karl's always picking my mom up on the weekends, leaving her Mazda parked in the garage. I don't know how likely it is she'll let me roll, but it's worth a shot. I may not be the reigning queen right now, but I'm still in the drama club and I'm making an appearance, come hell or high water.

"Okay, Miss Jackson, please find an open space and parallel park."

Damn, this was where I messed up last time. But practice makes perfect and I'm going to swing it.

I pull up next to a car parked in front of my mom's building, slightly passing it, just like I've seen my mom do a million times. Taking a deep breath, I shift the automatic gear into reverse, ready to jump over the final hurdle. I swing my right arm behind Tina's head, draping my arm behind the passenger's seat and slowly let my foot off the gas while turning the steering wheel ever so gently. I expertly park the car and return the gear to drive to straighten out the vehicle before shutting off the engine.

"Did I pass?" I eagerly ask, ready for my wings.

Tina scribbles something on the paper, ignoring my excitement. I'm sure she's tired of dealing with overzealous teenage drivers and I'm no exception. But after the week I've had, I need some good news and soon.

"Yes, you did. Merry Christmas." She passes me the yellow slip with my score and the word "pass" written across the top in big red letters. "Give this to the DMV when you go to take your test. Have a nice holiday."

"Thank you and you too." I take the paper from her before she gets out to reclaim the wheel. I grab my bags out of the backseat and hurry onto the curb because Tina looks ready to take off. I can tell by her paranoid body language that this white girl's uncomfortable in Inglewood and can't wait to get out of the hood.

I can't wait to tell my parents that I passed my Driver's Ed course, and the first person I'm calling is my daddy. If I have my way, I'll be the first one in line at the DMV in the morning and I'll drive myself to the cast party. Nothing's going to get in my way, not now.

My dad picked me up bright and early this morning, just like he said he would. I got my license, but no car to roll as of yet. My mom drove straight to work from Karl's house yesterday and won't be back until Sunday. But she wasn't completely closed to the idea of me driving her car one day. I'm just glad Jeremy's available to take me to the cast party, since this isn't really Rah's thing. And now that Chance and Nellie are an item, I can't ask him to take me. Whatever. As long as I get to show off and shake Laura up a bit, I don't care if I have to walk back to Redondo Beach to get there, as long as I make it.

When Jeremy and I arrive at Matt's house—the usual spot for our parties—the front lawn is packed with drama students and groupies alike. The first one I see is Nellie.

"Hey man," Jeremy says, giving his boy dap. Nellie looks at Jeremy and smiles before scowling at me.

What the hell?

"What's up, y'all?' Chance says, giving me a big hug. Nellie pulls Chance's arm, ready to go inside.

She's not going anywhere before I have my say. "So, what's up with you, Nellie? I see ASB has been working you like a slave, putting up new posters and all." My former friend looks at me hard like she wants to hit me, but I know Nellie knows better than that. She may have a new attitude, but she's the same old Nellie inside.

"Whatever. How are you, Jeremy?" Nellie asks.

I know she didn't just dismiss me and try to speak to my friend. Oh, she's really feeling herself now. Not wanting to get in the middle of our mess, Jeremy decides to exit stage right and greet Matt and Seth, who are also outside hanging out. The last time Nellie and I were here, we had a good time. But now, I wish she'd just leave.

"I'm good, Nellie. Jayd, I'll be over there when you're ready to go inside."

It's a typical Saturday night in Redondo, with all of the rich kids outside on their sprawling front lawns, bumping T.I. out of their state-of the-art sound systems in their fancy cars. Nellie's dreaming if she thinks she'll ever fit in here. She's also dreaming if she thinks I'm going to let her rude ass get away with ignoring me.

"Did you hear me greet you or is being rude also a personality requirement for running with Laura?"

Nellie looks down at me, finally ready to speak. "I'm sick of being the boogie bitch amongst the ghetto girls. And Mickey's shit is more foul than Misty's. I can't be a party to it anymore than you can be Misty's friend after what she put you through."

" 'Amongst, a party to,' " I say, mocking her proper diction. Our girl has always been prissy but this is a bit much, even for her. "Nellie, I don't know who put that stick so far up your ass, but I'll gladly remove it if you need me to."

Nellie looks like I just spilled grape juice on her favorite white Gucci blouse, and her tone is equally unforgiving. "Jayd, I don't know you or Mickey anymore. From this day on, consider yourself warned."

Warned about what? She can't do anything to me.

Nellie walks away, leaving a stunned Chance behind to follow his new master, but not before he talks to his old friend.

"I hate to be the one to tell you this, but someone's got to snap your girl back to reality," Chance says, walking me toward the main house while also following Nellie. Chance's heavy platinum chain shifts from one side of this thin chest to the other as we make our way slowly up the hill. I miss kicking it with my boy.

"What's up, Chance?"

He looks down at me, drapes his arm around my shoulders and takes a deep breath like what he's about to say is top secret. "Nellie doesn't know that I know this, so you can't tell her it came from me."

Oh, this must be good if Chance is swearing me to secrecy. I nod in agreement of our pact and let him continue.

"In order to be in their crew, the girls have to be hazed in different ways. Nellie already proved she could take one for the team twice by not fighting too hard when Laura spread that half-naked picture of her around campus, and again when Tania planted the nasty apple for her at the Masquerade Ball."

Ahead of us, Nellie stops at the main entrance of the lavish home, turning around and facing us several feet behind her, well out of normal earshot. But she knows by our body language that something's up.

"And why do I care?" I take Chance's arm, turning him

away from Nellie's gaze, just in case her eyes are anything like Esmeralda's piercing stares.

"All she has to do now is give up a secret about a former best friend—or two, in this case."

"What secret, exactly, did she give up?" I ask. The look on Chance's face is all the answer I need. "She told them about Mickey ditching with Nigel and having me sign her note, didn't she?" So all this time I was right about Nellie selling us out. It's amazing how low a person will sink to be a part of whatever they consider to be the "in" crowd. And Nellie's standards just keep sinking lower and lower.

"Chance, I'm waiting," Nellie says, impatiently crossing her arms over her flat chest and tapping her left foot.

I can't wait to put my foot up her ass, but this isn't the time or the place.

"You coming, Jayd?" Chance asks, not moving from where we're standing, but obviously knowing his limits with Nellie.

I look across the yard at Jeremy, who gives me a look like he's not feeling this party at all. And honestly, neither am I. I look around the property and neither Laura nor Reid's car is here, which means they haven't arrived yet, if they're coming at all. They're not part of the drama club and may not show, which means I'll have to wait until Monday to test out the spray on Laura anyway. Why not save the night and chill with Jeremy? I do have a driver's license to celebrate.

"Nah, I think me and Jeremy have other plans." I don't know what they are yet, but anything beats being here and having to deal with Nellie's twisted ass for the remainder of a perfectly good evening.

"You can't leave yet. I've got a little something for you," Chance says, pulling a small wrapped gift out of his jacket pocket. Jeremy, seeing the exchange, walks over to see what's in the package. Nellie looks shocked at Chance's surprise: I guess Chance isn't completely lost under her spell.

"Oh, Chance," I say, unwrapping the pretty, antique brass picture frame with the original Macbeth flyer behind the glass. It's nice to see my name listed in the lead role again. "This is the most thoughtful gift I've ever received."

"You'll always be a queen to me," he says, hugging me and making Nellie steam with jealousy. Jeremy doesn't look too happy about the gift either, but he doesn't look as upset as Nellie does. Wait until Monday rolls around and I'm really back in the lead, not just on paper. I can mold my reality into anything I want it to be. Nellie and the rest of my haters will be there to witness who's got the real power to stop a show around here.

~ 12 ~
The Showstopper

"One night only/
There's nothing more to say."

—BEYONCÉ/*DREAMGIRLS*

After all of Saturday's excitement, I opted for a quiet re-mainder of my weekend. I braided Rah's hair Sunday afternoon, as agreed. Afterwards he brought me back to Mama's house early so I could get some work done in the spirit room while Mama was at the shelter. Daddy spent all day at church, which isn't unusual, and I took the opportunity to take another quiet bath and get to bed early for a change.

Now, I can't wait until opening night tonight. Laura won't know what hit her—literally. She thinks she's got my crown in the bag, but she's got another think coming. And I'll be right there tonight to make sure she gets everything she deserves.

"Bryan, out," I whisper through the closed bathroom door. I don't want to risk missing my bus and this morning we're both running late.

"Patience, young blood," he says through the door. "It sounds like someone's nervous about their opening night. Is this how all divas act?"

"Bryan, not today," I plead. "I've got to get ready." He opens the door slowly, tempting me to kick it in and push him out of my way. But I choose to wait. I'll have to exercise a lot of patience today, so I might as well start off on the right foot.

"What's the rush? The play isn't until later tonight."

I'm surprised anyone in this household knows my extra-curricular activity schedule. Not a single one of them has ever come to any of my events, especially not a play. It's just not my family's cup of tea.

"Yes, but I've got business to handle before then."

He opens the door to see me standing in the hallway, holding all of my morning essentials and looking desperate, which is exactly how I feel. Sensing that I'm talking about more than catching my bus, he gathers his things without subjecting me to any more torture.

"You'll be alright, little Jayd," Bryan says, removing a wet towel from his head and leaving the bathroom. "You've got that hustler in you. Trust me, when it comes down to the moment of truth, you'll know what to do and how to do it. That's a real hustler, baby, and it's in your blood. Now go on and get before you're late for school. Don't have me get my belt out."

I love Bryan. He always knows what to say and when to say it. Mama says that one of his deities is also Legba and I can tell. He's always got my back and clears the road for me whenever I need it.

"Thank you," I say, entering the steamy bathroom. I should've put my shower cap on before coming in here. I don't want to mess up my hair before my big night. All the spray in the world can't straighten my hair out once the frizz gets to it.

"Anytime."

Now I can get ready for my day. Before I can even get to drama class, I have to deal with turning in my paper in government class and with the rest of my school day. I just hope it goes by smoothly and that I get to be in the same room with Laura before we go on stage. All I need is one moment and I'll have my crown back in no time.

*   *   *

When I arrive on campus, the air is thick with excitement on various levels. It's the last week of school before the long break and opening night for the festival. The athletes and cheerleaders are gearing up for their performance in the festival, as well as the other side acts. But the main attraction is always the play. This is one of the few times the drama club gets to shine. We will perform for three nights in a row, with tonight being the biggest performance of all, and it's mine for the taking. All I have to do is get through this day, and it starts by making it through third period.

"Good morning, class," Mr. Adewale says, walking in and making my day instantly brighten. Jeremy's not here yet and, with the bell ringing as Mr. A speaks, I don't think he's going to show. "Mrs. Peterson will be out until after the holiday. Your papers will be due when she returns."

Now, that's the kind of luck I'm talking about. Mr. A smiles at me. He knows he's given me the best gift I could've received around here.

"You are the man," I say, walking up to the teacher's desk to flirt a little before we start our day.

"I didn't do anything. She's got a cold." He looks up from his usual pile of work momentarily, giving me a slight wink.

"Well, thank you for being here. Your presence is always helpful." Mr. A looks so cute with his dreads hanging over his shoulders instead of pulled back in his usual ponytail.

"I'm glad I could help. By the way, did you get that situation straightened out you were dealing with last week?"

"Not yet, but it's all good. Let's just say I have a little something up my sleeve."

"I have no doubt that you do," he says.

Mr. A's tone gives me the same chill I got on Tuesday when he gave me the advice to hold my ground. What's up with Mr. Adewale's vibe towards me?

"Now get back to your seat and polish up that paper. I know it could use a little more work." He passes me the papers I assume he intended to give me the other day. I'll check this information out and do more research on the man himself during the two-week break. But right now, he's right. I have other things to focus on. Tonight's drama is at the top of my list.

It's after school and everyone in the drama room is so excited about the play that the noise level makes it difficult for anyone to hear a word that Mrs. Sinclair's yelling over our heads. We're all running around like chickens with our heads cut off and Laura's nowhere in sight. But, like all chickens, she'll have to show her neck sometime.

"Okay kids, listen up. I need all of the boys on stage for a final costume fitting. Girls, get your hair and makeup done. You're on in five." Because my costumes had to be altered again, I still get to wear my original nightgown intended for Lady Macbeth's sleepwalking scene. It's a plain, beige floor-length dress and it looks better than the gown they gave Laura to wear.

"Poor Jayd," Laura says, occupying the seat next to mine at the long dressing vanity. I'm glad she's finally decided to show. "Always a bridesmaid and never the bride," she says, primping in the mirror.

Now's the perfect time to spray my "Hustler's Luck" potion and rid myself of her evil energy once and for all.

"Not everyone's trying to get hitched," I say, taking the small bottle out of my purse and placing it on the vanity. I eye the simple, plastic bottle before picking it up and lightly spraying the floral scent over my head and then over the rest of my body.

"That smells nice," Alia says.

I almost didn't recognize her because her witch's costume

is perfect. She, China, and the new girl, Shawn, make the best witches ever. Laura was also supposed to play a witch until she took my part. Luckily, China volunteered because I wasn't going to take up that broom. I'm nobody's witch, not even in a play.

"Thank you. I like it, too. What do you think, Laura?"

Ready to make a smart-ass remark, Laura tries to speak, but nothing comes out of her mouth. Laura looks panic-stricken at her silent reflection in the mirror.

You, she mouths at me as I smile victoriously at her reflection.

What's she going to do? Run and tell on me? Not today she's not, and this is the only moment that matters. As we say in the theater, the show must go on. It stops for no one, Laura included.

"Laura, what's wrong?" Alia walks over to Laura, noticing her falling tears. "I'll go get Mrs. Sinclair."

Just then our teacher walks in, accompanied by Ms. Toni and Mrs. Bennett, who look equally concerned.

"What's going on here?" Mrs. Sinclair walks up to Laura, who is now completely beside herself.

I stay in my seat, eyeing my reflection and watching the tragic scene unfold. Laura tries to speak, pointing at me and mimicking me spraying myself and then losing her voice. She's actually improving in her acting skills. I'm glad her being my understudy paid off in some way other than Laura taking my role. Damn, Mama's good with her shit.

"I don't know what she said, but this isn't good," Ms. Toni says, looking from me to Laura, not believing what she's witnessing. I know she's heard about my powers, too. And after tonight's unlikely event, I know Ms. Toni's got about a thousand questions for me.

"I just thank God Jayd knows the part through and through. We don't have time to figure this out right now. We have a show to put on in an hour. Matt, Seth, where's Jayd's original costume? Cast change!" Mrs. Sinclair yells. Her curly red hair is bushier than usual, which means she's really at her wits' end with this production. Working with Mrs. Bennett can stress anyone out. But it's showtime and Mrs. Sinclair's in charge now.

"You won't get away with this," Mrs. Bennett mouths at my reflection in the mirror.

I would respond, but I know my power and I don't need to prove a thing to her. Mrs. Sinclair takes the beautiful, red velvet gown out of the plastic cover it's been trapped in all week. Now, that's royalty.

"Here's your crown, Jayd," Seth says, handing the small tiara to me.

Before I can properly secure it to my head, Laura reaches up, snatching it from my head just as my dream predicted.

"Get off me, trick," I yell, fighting Laura for what is rightfully mine in the first place.

"Stop it, you two. We don't have time for this! We have a show to put on," Mrs. Sinclair yells. Ms. Toni separates us while Mrs. Bennett looks on in disbelief. I bet she didn't see this one coming, but I did and I'm glad for it.

"Amateur," Seth says exasperatedly toward Laura as she's escorted from the room, kicking and not screaming. He has no patience for people who don't take his theater seriously.

"What happened?" Chance asks. But seeing me heading toward the dressing room with my costume in hand, he already knows. "I don't know how you did it, but I knew you could," he says, hugging me before returning to the stage.

I'm ready to wear my crown and own my part. Let Laura come at me again and I'll show her who's really boss. But for now, I'll be happy playing my role.

* * *

The past two nights have been unbelievable. We received standing ovations at each of the sold-out shows and tonight will be no exception.

"Hello, Laura. Still speechless, I see," I say to a mute Laura as I pass her by, entering the main hall.

It's the last day of school and I want to make sure I have all of my books before Rah comes to pick me up this afternoon. We're going to have an early dinner before my final performance tonight. He's been to every show and so has Jeremy, who was absent from school again today. I don't know how many times he can get his mom to sign sick notes, but I guess the rules are different for students like him and students like Mickey and Nigel.

"I'll get you for this," Laura mouths at me, shooting daggers at me with her brown eyes.

"You really shouldn't ride around with the top down on your car during the winter, no matter how cute you think you look. You never know how the changing seasons will affect your health." I know she wants to tell everyone about how I caused her to lose her voice, but it's a mute point now. I never confessed to the forgery and they can't prove a thing. They may have been able to get Nellie to join their forces and even get Mickey in trouble, but I'm not the one. When will they learn not to mess with me?

"Hey Jayd," Mickey says, coming out of the bathroom before Laura can leave. Nellie also enters the crowded hall from the ASB room, not far from where Mickey's standing. I can't stand it anymore. My girls need to come back together, damn Laura and her crew.

"Nellie, you're being hustled. Laura's just using you until she gets bored. Can't you recognize a pimp when you see one?"

"Don't listen to her, Nellie," Laura whispers. She's slightly more audible than on opening night but not much.

What is she, Nellie's life coach now?

"You're nothing but their little token black girl for their crew. Tania's spot needed to be filled. They're not your real friends, Nellie. We are."

"Speak for yourself," Mickey says, looking at Nellie and rolling her neck like only a sistah can.

"Well, I'd rather be the token black girl in Laura's crew than the token bourgie in the gangster girl posse," Nellie says, walking through the steady stream of students and joining Laura.

Now I know for fact that Nellie's lost her damned mind, calling me gangster. No doubt, I'm straight hood. But being a gangster girl is Mickey's mantra, not mine.

"Oh, Nellie, please don't get it twisted. I will slap the shit out of you if you keep talking to me crazy like that," I say, ready to snap her delusional ass back into reality. What kind of magic has Laura worked on our girl?

"Jayd, just leave it alone," Mickey says, walking over to hold me back. At least one of my homegirls still has my back. "As far as I'm concerned, Laura can have her wanna-be-white ass. I've got all I need right here," Mickey says, holding my arm while she rubs her baby bump. Nellie's hair should be as green as a shamrock, as jealous as she appears to be right now. "Keep her. Maybe she'll be a better friend to y'all then she has been to us."

I hate to admit defeat, but I'm with Mickey on this one. When it's time to move on, there's no stopping the motion. And I think Nellie's on the same path. I just hope our paths don't collide, leaving us all hurt in the end.

Epilogue

I'm glad Bryan decided to add iPods to his parking lot hustle. Otherwise, I'd probably never buy myself one and I stopped making Christmas lists when I was a little girl. He sold it to me for twenty dollars, so I just braided his hair up for free. When we can't buy, we barter. And since my mom's car doesn't have a radio, I needed to do something. A girl can't keep it moving without her iTunes, for real.

"I like your iPod, Miss Jackson," Rah says, pulling up to my mom's house just as I'm ready to go inside. It's Christmas Eve and I don't want to be late or my mom will leave me high and dry. I've already wasted enough time chilling with Jeremy all day at the beach. Rah must have me on radar because his timing is perfect and I'm glad he's here. Mama's going to be so happy to see him tonight. It's been years since Rah accompanied me to a family dinner.

"Why, thank you," I say, pulling the headset out of my ears and turning it off before stopping in my tracks. "Bryan's selling them behind Miracle Market if you want to pick one up."

Rah parks his car on the street. Karl's SUV is parked across the street, so I know my mom's ready to roll. She wants to get this first meeting between her boyfriend and her mother over and done with as soon as possible.

"Bryan's always got a side hustle," Rah says, smiling at my uncle's business prowess. "I know that nigga will never be broke. I just ran into him around the corner from my grandmother's house, but he didn't tell me about his latest venture."

"I wasn't sure if you were meeting me here or at Mama's, since you were already on that side of town," I say, realizing Rah technically shouldn't be here. "I thought you were meeting Sandy at your grandmother's and bringing Rahima to Mama's. I'll run up and tell my mother you're here and she and Karl can go on ahead of us, cool?"

Rah catches up to me speed walking up the concrete pavement, and stops me. "Jayd, I'm sorry baby."

Oh, no. Anytime he begins with that line, I know it's not going to end well.

"But Sandy wants me to come all the way out to Pomona to get Rahima and I don't have a choice. I've got to go." Rah looks sad as he breaks the news to me. He lifts my chin up so he can look me in the eyes as he breaks my heart, again. But this time, my sweetness has just about run out.

"Why do I always feel like I'm on borrowed time with you?" I know I'm being a bit selfish, but really. How many times are my plans going to be affected by him and his issues?

"Jayd, come on. You know I want to come with you." Rah takes me by the hand, but I'm feeling very unsympathetic at the moment. This holiday season has sucked since Halloween, and I'm tired of it. I'm getting one thing I want in total this time around. And what I want is to be the priority when it comes to the girls in Rah's life, not including his daughter, of course.

"Then come. You can pick up Rahima tomorrow or later on tonight. Stop jumping through Sandy's hoops and she'll stop throwing them out there." I know my words seem a little insensitive, but enough is enough. It's time for some tough love.

"Jayd, are y'all coming or what?" my mom asks as she and Karl step down the stairs, ready to roll. They look cute in matching black suits, my mom's, of course, much more fierce than his dapper attire. But Karl looks just as good in my eyes. They make a handsome couple.

"You look nice, Ms. Jackson," Rah says. "Hi, I'm Rah," he says, shaking Karl's hand.

My mom looks into my red eyes and can read my mind without invading my thoughts. "Should we wait for you or do you have a ride?"

Rah looks at me again as Karl and my mom wait for an answer. His sad, puppy-dog look says "sorry," but I'm still not feeling his pain.

"Can y'all please wait? I'll only be a minute." I look at Rah and shake my head. He knows he's really got to get his stuff together because I wait for no one.

"I'll call you later if I can make it by. Tell Mama I said hello," Rah says to my back as I sprint upstairs to quickly wash my face and change into something a little nicer than my beach attire.

My motto for the New Year is to keep it moving, no matter what. I'm not waiting for anyone to help me meet my goals. Dealing with Laura's vengeful ass has taught me to be one step ahead of the competition at all times. And as long as I keep my hustle tight, no one can stop my flow—best friends, boyfriends and enemies alike. I'm going to keep it moving and, this time around, I'm not slowing down for anyone.

Drama High, Volume 7:
HUSTLIN'

L. Divine

ABOUT THIS GUIDE

The following questions are intended to
enhance your group's reading of
DRAMA HIGH: HUSTLIN'
by L. Divine.

DISCUSSION QUESTIONS

1. What is your definition of a hustler? Is it a good or bad thing? Explain your answer.
2. Should Jayd accept her father's help and ignore Mama's, Netta's and her mom's warnings? What would you do?
3. Should Rah take care of Sandy because she has his daughter? Should Jeremy continue to do the same for Tania?
4. Do you know any gold diggers? How do you know they're gold diggers? What's the difference between a gold digger and a regular girlfriend?
5. Should Jayd try to save Nellie from herself or let her suffer the consequences of her decisions? What would a good friend do?
6. Should Rahima live with Sandy or Rah? Is Sandy a good mother? Is Rah a good father? Explain.
7. Should Jayd sell out Nigel and Mickey to save herself? What would you do in her situation?
8. Do you like Shakespeare? How do you envision Jayd as Lady Macbeth? Is she believable?
9. Why do you think Mickey's man is on Jayd's case? How would you advise Jayd to handle the situation?
10. If you could make a multi-use potion, what would it be for? What form would you make it in (spray, balm, etc.)?

11. If you were Nellie and Jeremy, would you be jealous of Chance and Jayd's relationship? Why or why not?

12. Why is Mrs. Bennett so hard on Jayd? Do you know, or know of, any teachers like her?

13. Is Nellie right about the way she feels about Mickey? Would you have reacted the same way if you were Mickey? Explain.

Stay tuned for the next book in
the DRAMA HIGH series,
KEEP IT MOVIN'

Until then, satisfy your DRAMA HIGH craving
with the following excerpt from the next
exciting installment.

ENJOY!

Prologue

As I stand here listening to Rah's rationale about why he has to leave me stranded with no date, so he can drive all the way out to Pomona to meet Sandy's crazy ass, I can feel my head getting hot. I now know the heat of a thousand suns. The tears well up behind my tired eyes, but I refuse to let him hear me cry. I haven't even made it into the bathroom yet and I already want to throw my cell in the toilet and flush the bull Rah's feeding me.

"Jayd, did you hear what I just said?" Rah asks, responding to my silence.

I put the lid down and take a seat on the toilet, slowly removing my beach attire from my afternoon out with Jeremy. I was in a great mood before Rah burst my bubble. Now the last thing I feel like doing is going to a party. I'm not in the mood to celebrate a damn thing unless it has something to do with Rah's exes Sandy and Trish disappearing from our lives for good.

"I'm sorry about this, baby. I'm going to get there and back as fast as I can."

"It's all good, Rah. No worries." The untruthful words are barely audible to me, so I know he didn't hear me. Every time he pulls this shit I tell myself it'll be the last time, just like the last time. When will too much finally be enough?

"If there was another way, I'd do it in a heartbeat." Rah sighs deeply through the phone and I can feel his frustration. I wish he were stronger in his stance with both Sandy and Trish. Maybe I should have made the Bitter Bwoy Brew I concocted to repel his broads to work on myself instead. This boy's drama is starting to drain me and I'm tired of being his willing victim. "You believe me, don't you, baby?"

"I believe you think you're doing the right thing and that's all that matters."

"I don't like the sound of that," Rah says, while I finish undressing and fill the sink with warm water, ready to wash up and get back downstairs.

I can feel my mom's impatience and I know she's about to give me a psychic earful if I don't hurry up. She wasn't planning on being my ride this evening and I know she has other plans with Karl, which means I'm cramping her style.

"Well, what do you expect? You not only threw off my day, you also threw off my mother and Karl's plans as well. But like I said, no worries. You've got to go handle your business and so do I. I'll talk to you later." I abruptly end our phone conversation. I need to get all of my tears out and keep it moving if I'm going to make it through the holidays. Otherwise, I'll be stuck in this love quicksand indefinitely and I can't afford to stop for anyone, Rah included.

~ 1 ~
Keep It Movin'

"Keep on moving/
Don't stop like the hands of time."

—SOUL II SOUL

"*Jayd, hurry up and get down here. We've got to get going if Karl and I are going to make it to Mama's dinner in time enough to leave early. We're going to a party at Karl's brother's house afterwards and I don't want to get there too late.*"

Leave it to my mom to have an exit plan for a family dinner.

"*I heard that, young lady. What happened with Rah? We already have to take you home unexpectedly and that's going to take up even more of our time to be together.*"

Why does my mom have to sweat my mind while I'm rushing to get dressed? She can wait another ten minutes and I'll be downstairs in the car with her and Karl, where she'll be able to grill me all the way to Compton.

"He had to go get his little girl," I mutter, still in shock that Rah has left me stranded for yet another holiday. What is it with him and all the other broads in his life? How come they can snap their fingers and Rah comes running, usually leaving me behind in the dust? I'm the one he supposedly loves, but what I want always comes last. What the hell?

"*Well, I don't understand what that has to do with him*

not coming to Mama's, but whatever. Did you tell him he could bring his daughter? I know Mama would love to see the baby."

"Mom, can this wait until I'm out of the bathroom, please? I'm trying to wash my face and I still have to pick out an outfit to wear."

I didn't want to cry in front of my mom because she would tease me to no end. She's always viewed shedding tears as a weakness, especially if they're falling over a dude. But I can't hold them in any longer, especially not now that I'm looking in the mirror. I trace the tracks of my tears down my cheeks, washing them away in the gentle lather. I wish I could wash away the pain behind them just as easily.

"I already picked out your attire. You're wearing the red dress hanging in my bathroom doorway. Merry Christmas. The shoes are already by the front door. Now hurry up and get down here. We've got to keep it moving, Jayd, no matter how tough shit is. Suck it up."

"Mom, I'm coming," I say aloud, even if technically I am the only one in the apartment. How am I supposed to concentrate on being jolly with Christmas spirit when the one I want to be with is going to be with someone else—again? Having to give up spending turkey day with Rah to Trish and her brother was one thing. But Rah passing up Mama's Christmas Eve dinner to meet up with his baby-mama is more than I can take.

"Jayd, haven't you figured out that the moment you stop taking Rah's mess will be the moment he stops dishing it out? You should know better by now."

"That's exactly what I said to Rah about Sandy and her games. She's playing him, and every time Rah participates in her drama, he's letting her get away with it."

I quickly rinse the mango-apricot face scrub from my cheeks before filling the sink with warm water to quickly wash up. I wish I had time to take a shower, but knowing my mom, she'll leave me if I waste any more of her time.

"Well, it's time to start following your own advice. And the sooner the better, because at the rate you're going, Rah's going to be a distant memory if you don't step up your game. I remember Sandy being a train wreck and if that's how she looks in my memory, I can only imagine what she must look like in your rearview."

"You can only imagine; since when?" I ask, washing the salty ocean residue off my body, ready to slip into my new dress and my mom's shoes, but not before I butter up with some of Mama's Egyptian musk body butter. I only wear the good stuff on special occasions and Mama's creations are the best.

"Jayd, I do allow you some privacy, don't I? I don't want to relive your memories, trust me. What I see in your little head is more than enough. Now, get down here. You've got five minutes."

I exit the bathroom and eye the full-length fitted dress hanging in my mother's doorway. Damn, she's got great taste. The Chinese inspired design of the dress makes it that much more stunning and gives it a classic appearance.

"I thought you'd like it. Don't forget to wear panty hose or Mama will flip out on both of us. Make it quick, Jayd."

"I'll be right down." As usual, the beach air has made my fresh press frizzy, so a slicked-back ponytail will have to do. I'll have to hook my hair up later on tonight or in the morning if I'm too tired from this evening's festivities. Mama usually has a full evening of activities planned for everyone to participate in. She loves to play games like Taboo and Pictionary to get the entire family involved. Mama also makes us

choose teams, especially since she and Daddy are always the team captains. Any chance she has to beat Daddy at any game, Mama's taking.

"Nah, nah nahnah. Wait till I get my money right." Kanye serenades Jeremy's incoming call. Damn, I don't have time for any more drama today and I just left him less than thirty minutes ago. What could he possibly want now?

"Hey, Jeremy. What's up?" I ask, propping the phone up to my ear with my right shoulder while squeezing into my outfit. I've gained some weight between the holidays and won't be slimming back down until after the winter break. I hope my mom doesn't say anything about me stretching my gift out. It seems like she never gains weight, no matter how much she eats.

"What's up is you," he says, his voice as husky as ever. Damn, he sounds so sexy over the phone. "You want to go out tonight? My friends are having a little get-together at the beach and they asked about you."

I know that means his surfing buddies, who will undoubtedly be as high as kites and Jeremy will no doubt be flying right along with them.

"Thank you, but no thank you," I say, putting my heels on before heading out the door. I take a quick glance in the mirror, realizing I have on no lip gloss or eye shadow, making me appear plain in this gorgeous dress. I also need something to cover my arms in these short sleeves or else I'm going to freeze my behind off.

"Grab a jacket and let's get, little Jayd. You can primp in the car," my mom insists impatiently.

I grab my mom's shawl from the coat rack, along with my purse, and I'm finally ready to leave. It's after five now and I know Mama's waiting on us before serving dinner.

"I promise I'll stay sober," Jeremy says, missing my point

completely. "I really enjoyed kicking it with you today and I'm not ready for it to end."

"Jeremy, I already told you I have plans with my family," I say, slamming the door shut behind me as I run down the stairs. I can see my mom's pissed look from all the way across the street. I bet she could kill someone with one of her looks if she tried hard enough.

"Don't play about that, Jayd. Ever," my mom says, way too seriously. I wonder what that's all about.

"Well, then invite me to come to dinner at your house for a change. I'll be happy to escort you, that is unless there's already someone else on your arm?"

Oh yeah, that'll go over real well, me bringing my white ex-boyfriend to Christmas dinner at Mama's, even if my original date did stand me up.

"Why not? Enjoy yourself, Jayd. And you know Mama loves company on Christmas Eve. This would be the best time to bring Jeremy if you plan on keeping him around, even if I do disapprove of the little white boy. But at least he's cute and treats you well. And if he meets you there he can take you home and me and Karl can keep it moving like we originally planned. So tell him to meet you there and get your ass in this truck now, or he'll be picking you up from here, too."

"You know what, Jeremy?" I say, swinging the heavy door of the large SUV open before tossing my Lucky bag onto the seat. I always have to pull myself up high into these large vehicles, messing my dress up and causing me to work too hard. I wish Karl drove his Camry instead of the Expedition today. I don't like riding in large trucks. "Why don't you meet me there and then we can go out. Cool?"

"Very," he says. I can hear his smile through the phone. As

long as Rah has other interests, so will I, even if he is the only ex I want to really be with for Christmas. But like Mama says, gifts may not always come in the packaging I want, but I always get just what I need. I just hope she understands that when I show up with Jeremy instead of Rah.

"I must be the luckiest man this holiday, with the two prettiest women in all of LA riding in my car," Karl says while I settle into his ride. He pulls away from the curb and heads toward the 405 freeway, which will lead us to the 91, the quickest way to Mama's side of Compton from Inglewood. I'm going to have to learn all of the routes since I'll be driving soon. If I get my hustle on over the break, I'll have more than enough to make a nice down payment on something small and economical. With the high gas prices, I know Karl must be regretting buying this ride.

"*That's why he got the Toyota to drive during the week. The truck is his weekend car,*" my mom says, psychically defending her man. And I don't blame her. My salty mood is no excuse for me talking about him. Karl's a sweetie, even if he is twice our size, and he's good to my mom. What more can a sistah ask for?

"So young lady, what did you ask Santa for this year?"

I like that Karl makes small talk with me without much effort. When I talk to my daddy, it's like pulling teeth without novocaine.

"A car," I say. My phone, now on vibrate, signals a text from Rah. I'm through crying over his ass.

Hey baby. I'm sorry about how this day turned out. I'll try and make it back as soon as I can. I love you girl. Don't be mad at me for too long and holla at your boy when you get a min.

"Well, I think every teenager has the same thing on her list," Karl continues, taking my mind away from Rah and back to my list. A loyal boyfriend's also on the list, but I think that's too much to ask for, even from Santa. "Anything more affordable?"

Is he asking because he's making small talk or because he wants to get me a gift? None of my mom's men have ever bought me anything directly.

"Cash always works," I say, just in case this is more than an innocent probe. I can use all the dividends I can get my hands on.

"That's my girl," my mom says, gently rubbing Karl's hand lying on the armrest. If I didn't know better, I'd say they've been in love forever. Hard to believe they've only been dating for a couple of months. "No matter what they say, cash is still king in my wallet."

"So, you don't want the gold American Express card I got you with your name on it for Christmas?" Karl looks at my mom's eyes light up like a little girl on Christmas morning.

"Do I have to pay the bill?" My mom's nothing if not practical when it comes to her finances. Unlike other baby-mamas, her baby-daddy doesn't pay all of her bills. Mickey needs to come and spend the day with my mom to get a taste of what it's like being a single mother.

"What kind of gift would that be?" Karl exits the freeway, only a few minutes away from my grandparents' house. Remembering that Jeremy's never been all the way to my grandparents' house before, I send him a quick text with the address.

"Well then, hell yeah I want my card. Give it up," she says, patting him down like the police.

"I'll give it to you when we get to your mother's house. Back up, woman," he laughs, attempting to gently push my mom back down in her seat. But my mom's relentless in her quest. I hope Mama finds them as amusing as I do.

See you soon, Lady J.

Jeremy's text has all kinds of undertones in it. I know Jeremy wants us to get back together, but I'm not there. I hope he doesn't think his coming to Mama's house is a step in the direction of a relationship. Friends visit Mama too, and I have to make sure he understands that. The last thing I need is more drama with one of my exes.

START YOUR OWN BOOK CLUB

Courtesy of the DRAMA HIGH series

ABOUT THIS GUIDE

The following is intended to help you get
the book club you've always wanted
up and running!
Enjoy!

Start Your Own Book Club

A Book Club is not only a great way to make friends, but it is also a fun and safe environment for you to express your views and opinions on everything from fashion to teen pregnancy. A Teen Book Club can also become a forum or venue to air grievances and plan remedies for problems.

The People

To start, all you need is yourself and at least one other person. There's no criteria for who this person or persons should be other than them having a desire to read and a commitment to discuss things during a certain time frame.

The Rules

Just as in Jayd's life, sometimes even Book Club discussions can be filled with much drama. People tend to disagree with each other, cut each other off when speaking, and take criticism personally. So, there should be some ground rules:

1. Do not attack people for their ideas or opinions.
2. When you disagree with a book club member on a point, disagree respectfully. This means that you do not denigrate other people for their ideas or even their ideas themselves, i.e., no name calling or saying, "That's stupid!" Instead, say, "I can respect your position, however, I feel differently."
3. Back up your opinions with concrete evidence, either from the book in question or life in general.
4. Allow every one a turn to comment.
5. Do not cut a member off when the person is speaking. Respectfully wait your turn.
6. Critique only the idea. Do not criticize the person.

7. Every member must agree to and abide by the ground rules.

Feel free to add any other ground rules you think might be necessary.

The Meeting Place

Once you've decided on members, and agreed to the ground rules, you should decide on a place to meet. This could be the local library, the school library, your favorite restaurant, a bookstore, or a member's home. Remember, though, if you decide to hold your sessions at a member's home, the location should rotate to another member's home for the next session. It's also polite for guests to bring treats when attending a Book Club meeting at a member's home. If you choose to hold your meetings in a public place, always remember to ask the permission of the librarian or store manager. If you decide to hold your meetings in a local bookstore, ask the manager to post a flyer in the window announcing the Book Club to attract more members if you so desire.

Timing Is Everything

Teenagers of today are all much busier than teenagers of the past. You're probably thinking, "Between chorus rehearsals, the Drama Club, and oh yeah, my job, when will I ever have time to read another book that doesn't feature Romeo and Juliet!" Well, there's always time, if it's time well-planned and time planned ahead. You and your Book Club can decide to meet as often or as little as is appropriate for your bustling schedules. *Once a month* is a favorite option. *Sleepover Book Club* meetings—if you're open to excluding one gender—is also a favorite option. And in this day of high-tech, savvy teens, *Internet Discussion Groups* are also an appealing option. Just choose what's right for you!

Well, you've got the people, the ground rules, the place, and the time. All you need now is a book!

The Book

Choosing a book is the most fun. HUSTLIN' is of course an excellent choice, and since it's a series, you won't soon run out of books to read and discuss. Your Book Club can also have comparative discussions as you compare the first book, THE FIGHT, to the second, SECOND CHANCE, and so on.

But depending upon your reading appetite, you may want to veer outside of the Drama High series. That's okay. There are plenty of options, many of which you will be able to find under the Dafina Books for Young Readers Program in the coming months.

But don't be afraid to mix it up. Nonfiction is just as good as fiction and a fun way to learn about from where we came without just using a history text book. Science fiction and fantasy can be fun, too!

And always, always research the author. You might find the author has a website where you can post your Book Club's questions or comments. The author may even have an e-mail address available so you can correspond directly. Authors might also sit in on your Book Club meetings, either in person, or on the phone, and this can be a fun way to discuss the book as well!

The Discussion

Every good Book Club discussion starts with questions. HUS-TLIN', as does every book in the Drama High series, comes with a Reading Group Guide for your convenience, though of course, it's fine to make up your own. Here are some sample questions to get started:

1. What's this book all about anyway?
2. Who are the characters? Do we like them? Do they remind us of real people?
3. Was the story interesting? Were real issues of concern to you examined?
4. Were there details that didn't quite work for you or ring true?
5. Did the author create a believable environment—one that you could visualize?
6. Was the ending satisfying?
7. Would you read another book from this author?

Record Keeper

It's generally a good idea to have someone keep track of the books you read. Often libraries and schools will hold reading drives where you're rewarded for having read a certain number of books in a certain time period. Perhaps a pizza party awaits!

Get Your Teachers and Parents Involved

Teachers and parents love it when kids get together and read. So involve your teachers and parents. Your Book Club may read a particular book whereby it would help to have an adult's perspective as part of the discussion. Teachers may also be able to include what you're doing as a Book Club in the classroom curriculum. That way, books you love to read, such as the Drama High ones, can find a place in your classroom alongside the books you don't love to read so much.

Resources

To find some new favorite writers, check out the following resources. Happy reading!

Young Adult Library Services Association
http://www.ala.org/ala/yalsa/yalsa.htm

Carnegie Library of Pittsburgh
Hip-Hop!
Teen Rap Titles
*http://www.carnegielibrary.org/teens/read/booklists/teen
rap.html*

TeensPoint.org
What Teens Are Reading
*http://www.teenspoint.org/reading_matters/book_list.asp?s
ort=5&list=274*

Teenreads.com
http://www.teenreads.com

Sacramento Public Library
Fantasy Reading for Kids
http://www.saclibrary.org/teens/fantasy.html

Book Divas
http://www.bookdivas.com

Meg Cabot Book Club
http://www.megcabotbookclub.com

HAVEN'T HAD ENOUGH?
CHECK OUT THESE GREAT SERIES
FROM DAFINA BOOKS!

DRAMA HIGH
by L. Divine
Follow the adventures of a young sistah who's learning life in the hood is nothing compared to life in high school.

THE FIGHT	SECOND CHANCE	JAYD'S LEGACY
ISBN: 0-7582-1633-5	ISBN: 0-7582-1635-1	ISBN: 0-7582-1637-8
FRENEMIES	LADY J	COURTIN' JAYD
ISBN: 0-7582-2532-6	ISBN: 0-7582-2534-2	ISBN: 0-7582-2536-9

BOY SHOPPING
by Nia Stephens
An exciting "you pick the ending" series that lets the reader pick Mr. Right.

BOY SHOPPING	LIKE THIS AND LIKE THAT	GET MORE
ISBN: 0-7582-1929-6	ISBN: 0-7582-1931-8	ISBN:0-7582-1933-4

DEL RIO BAY CLIQUE
by Paula Chase
A wickedly funny series that explores friendship, betrayal, and how far some people will go for popularity.

SO NOT THE DRAMA	DON'T GET IT TWISTED
ISBN: 0-7582-1859-1	ISBN: 0-7582-1861-3

PERRY SKKY JR.
by Stephanie Perry Moore
An inspirational series that follows the adventures of a high school football star as he balances faith and the temptations of teen life.

PRIME CHOICE	PRESSING HARD
ISBN: 0-7582-1863-X	ISBN: 0-7582-1872-9
PROBLEM SOLVED	PRAYED UP
ISBN: 0-7582-1874-5	ISBN: 0-7582-2538-5